Also by Jennifer Brown

Life on Mars

*How Lunchbox Jones Saved Me from Robots,
Traitors, and Missy the Cruel*

Pennybaker School Is Headed for Disaster

PENNYBAKER SCHOOL
IS REVOLTING

Peachtree

Jennifer Brown

illustrated by Marta Kissi

BLOOMSBURY
CHILDREN'S BOOKS
NEW YORK LONDON OXFORD NEW DELHI SYDNEY

BLOOMSBURY CHILDREN'S BOOKS
Bloomsbury Publishing Inc., part of Bloomsbury Publishing Plc
1385 Broadway, New York, NY 10018

BLOOMSBURY, BLOOMSBURY CHILDREN'S BOOKS, and the Diana logo
are trademarks of Bloomsbury Publishing Plc

First published in the United States of America in July 2018
by Bloomsbury Children's Books

Text copyright © 2018 by Jennifer Brown
Illustrations copyright © 2018 by Marta Kissi

Bloomsbury books may be purchased for business or promotional use. For information on
bulk purchases please contact Macmillan Corporate and Premium Sales Department at
specialmarkets@macmillan.com

Library of Congress Cataloging-in-Publication Data
Names: Brown, Jennifer, author.
Title: Pennybaker School is revolting / by Jennifer Brown.
Description: New York : Bloomsbury, 2018.
Summary: Strange things are happening at Pennybaker School for the Uniquely Gifted, and
sixth-grader Thomas Fallgrout must stage a revolution to set them right.
Identifiers: LCCN 2017049962
ISBN 978-1-68119-176-8 (hardcover) • ISBN 978-1-68119-177-5 (e-book)
Subjects: | CYAC: Gifted children—Fiction. | Boarding schools—Fiction. | Schools—Fiction. |
Friendship—Fiction. | Mystery and detective stories.
Classification: LCC PZ7.B814224 Pc 2018 | DDC [Fic]—dc23
LC record available at https://lccn.loc.gov/2017049962

Book design by Colleen Andrews
Typeset by Westchester Publishing Services
Printed and bound in the U.S.A. by Berryville Graphics Inc., Berryville, Virginia
2 4 6 8 10 9 7 5 3 1

All papers used by Bloomsbury Publishing Plc are natural, recyclable products made from
wood grown in well-managed forests. The manufacturing processes conform to the
environmental regulations of the country of origin.

To find out more about our authors and books visit www.bloomsbury.com and sign up for
our newsletters.

For Paige, Weston, and Rand
May you always embrace your unique gifts

PENNYBAKER SCHOOL

IS REVOLTING

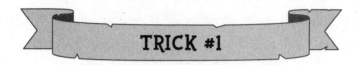

TRICK #1

THE PANTYHOSE PULL

I used to hate bow ties. That was before the pantyhose.

Mom insisted that they weren't pantyhose. She called them "stockings" and said that all the men in colonial times wore them.

But we were standing in the ladies' underwear section at the store when she said it, and she pulled the stockings off a shelf marked "Pantyhose" while we were surrounded by a bunch of old ladies all wearing pantyhose, and the plastic package had a picture of a woman wearing pantyhose right on the front.

So, yeah. Pantyhose.

The problem with pantyhose was they were impossible to get on. If I didn't pull hard enough, they fell down. If I pulled too hard, they ripped. And they were hot and itchy, and I wasn't sure Philadelphus Philadelphia even wore them. It was impossible to find a picture of Philadelphus Philadelphia anywhere.

I was still wrestling with my so-called stockings when Chip Mason came into my room. "Good day to you, Thomas Fallgrout!" he said, taking off his tricornered hat and bending low at the waist in a bow. "I bring glad tidings from Newburyport, Massachusetts."

Chip was my across-the-street neighbor, and my friend, too, even though he was weird and kind of annoying sometimes and I pretty much never understood what he was saying—especially when he was wearing his King's English socks. Chip had socks for every occasion. And I don't just mean Santa socks for Christmas and candy-corn socks for Halloween—Chip had socks for everything from movie night to geological studies.

Today, for the most part, Chip was dressed like me: coat, ruffled shirt, hat, pantyhose, shoes that made noise when you walked. Only his pantyhose weren't sagging around his ankles and didn't have holes in them.

"Who are you supposed to be?" I asked, giving mine another tug.

"John Pearson, of course," he said, bringing his heels together with a snap and saluting me.

"Soldier?"

"No, sir."

"Then why are you saluting me?"

He lowered his hand and clasped it behind his back with the other one. "I don't know. Seemed the right thing to do."

"Okay. So who was Pierce Johnson?"

"I don't know, who?"

I rolled my eyes. "I don't know! You're the one who decided to be him, not me!"

"My dear lad," Chip said, "the way you've

worded your declaration makes it sound as if I might have chosen to represent you for our assignment—which, of course, I could not do, as you are not a colonial figure of any sort. I believe your sentence structure would be clearer if you'd said something along the lines of *I didn't dress as Pierce Johnson; you did.* I have found that rewording things in my head a few times before saying them aloud helps to avoid confusion."

I opened my mouth to tell him how he could avoid the confusion of me putting him in a headlock, but he held up his hand to stop me.

"*However.* Given the context of our sentences previous, I imagine you meant to ask who 'John Pearson' was, for that is whose style of dress I'm meant to emulate. 'Pierce Johnson' is just some random gentleman who I'm sure is nice enough, but who is not a member of colonial society—although, without proper research, I cannot *definitively* make the claim that there were no Pierce Johnsons in colonial America. But going off the assumption that I am correct, and Pierce Johnson did not, indeed, exist in colonial society, he would not be appropriate for our assignment."

Our assignment. For Facts After the Fact class, otherwise known as History in a normal school. But Pennybaker School for the Uniquely Gifted was definitely not normal, and we didn't get normal assignments. The current non-normal assignment, called Act After the Fact, was to research and pretend to be a real-life but unknown colonial American citizen for one month.

One month of hot, itchy leg-stranglers.

Chip paced across my room, his hand tucked into his lapel. "It was quite the difficult decision, paring down the vast field of unsung heroes," he said. "Should I go for a humanitarian? A brave battlefield commander? A doctor? A scholar? There were just so many citizens to choose from."

There were? It had taken me three days to find a single one. That was the problem with unknown people—they were unknown. Then again, I wasn't Chip Mason. He was probably wearing his unknown colonial American citizen socks at the time.

"In the end, though," he said, "I chose inventor John Pearson."

"What did he invent?" I asked.

"Pearson's Pilot Bread!" he proclaimed proudly.

"Huh?"

"Sea biscuits?" he tried.

"I think your research might be wrong, Chip. Seabiscuit was a horse. Nobody invented a horse."

"Not true. The Greeks very much invented a horse when they wished to invade Troy."

I blinked. "Wait—this assignment is about Greece? And who is Troy?" More important question: Did Ancient Greek guys wear pantyhose?

Chip chose to ignore my questions. "Perhaps you've heard of it referred to as hardtack."

"What? The Greek horse?"

"No, not the—" He sighed and adjusted his proud posture again. "John Pearson was none other than the inventor of the fine and ever-enduring popular snack food . . ." He raised his arms dramatically. Chip did everything dramatically—almost as dramatically as my friend Wesley, the thespian. Chip would make a pretty good thespian, actually. He undoubtedly had thespian socks. "The cracker!"

"The cracker," I repeated. He nodded excitedly. "Out of all the colonial people in the world, you chose the dude who invented saltines?"

"Well, no. The inventor of saltines was actually—"

"Never mind. I don't want to know." I tugged on the pantyhose, and my big toe popped through the end. "Oh, come on," I said, pulling them off and wadding them up. I tossed them into the corner with the other nine hundred pairs I'd ruined. "Why do we have to wear all this, anyway?"

"The proper male colonial attire was a coat, breeches, a cravat—"

I pointed at him. "Nope. No way. I know what a cravat is. It's a tie. And if I have to wear pantyhose, I am not wearing a tie. Pick one end or the other."

"Spatterdashes," Chip said. I figured he meant something like "balderdash," a word Grandma Jo sometimes said when she thought something was ridiculous. But he stuck out one leg, swept his hand over it, and repeated, "Spatterdashes. Or leggings, if you prefer."

"Pantyhose," I grumbled, opening a new package.

"Not pantyhose." He thought about it. "Although possibly a predecessor to them. I must follow up with some research this evening during my post-school academic reflection."

I pulled the spatterdashes over my boxers, grabbed the breeches Mom had made for me, and yanked them up quickly. I haphazardly tucked in my usual white button-down school uniform shirt and covered it with a vest that Mom had made to match the breeches. I didn't look nearly as fancy as Chip did, and I certainly was not going to wear a cravat, but it would do.

There were three knocks on my door, and then Dad poked his head through. He was carrying his coffee, just like always, and his neck was red from shaving, also just like always.

"Hey, pal, you about ready to go?"

I shook one leg to make it stop itching. "No."

"Good. See you in ten minutes." He started to pull his head out of the doorway, and then stuck it back in. "Who are you supposed to be, Chip?"

"John Pearson."

Dad's face lit up. "Ah! The inventor of the illustrious cracker!"

"Indeed, my good man." Chip took off his hat and bowed low to the floor. "Indeed."

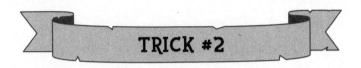

TRICK #2

THE DANCE DITCH

"It's about time, Thomas Fallgrout!" a pair of feet said to me.

I looked down to where normal feet should have been and saw Clover Prentice's scowling face. She dropped out of her handstand and into a forward roll, then stood up. Her forehead was kind of sweaty and red, probably from having been upside down for so long. Or maybe inside out. You never really knew with Clover. Her unique gift was contortionism. As Grandma Jo liked to say, she could tie herself up like a pretzel and dip herself in cheese. I wasn't sure what the cheese part was about. Probably Grandma Jo was just hungry when she said it.

"Sorry I'm late, Clover."

"Late?" She wound an arm around her neck and looked at her watch. "How about very, very late?" As if to agree with her, the warning bell rang, and everyone started climbing the giant staircase to their classrooms. "This is the third time this week you didn't get here early enough to polish her, and now her nostrils look dusty." She waved at the giant bust of Helen Heirmauser, revered math teacher from days of Pennybaker past. I had a love-hate relationship with that statue, after everything that happened when I first transferred to Pennybaker

School. I also had a love-hate relationship with my polishing duty. On one hand, it was an honor to be the school hero appointed to such an important task. On the other hand, it was a chore that involved getting to school early to spend up-close-and-personal time with the creepiest human head in all of human-head history. "It's my job as hall monitor to make sure the school is presenting its best face at all times," Clover continued.

"Well, if that's our best face, I'd hate to see our worst," I said, pointing at the goggle-eyed, openmouthed, wild-haired statue. I cracked myself up, but Clover simply stared at me.

"She's not shiny," she said. "And if you're not going to keep her polished, we'll just have to find someone else who will."

"Excuse me, my lady." Off with the hat again. If Chip wasn't careful, he was going to break himself in half from bowing so much. "I would be honored to take care of this glorious icon here. Cleanliness, after all, is next to Heirmauseriness."

I rolled my eyes. "You've got to be kidding."

He looked at me. "I never kid about hygiene, Thomas. You should know that."

Clover looked half-angry—at me—and half in love with Chip. Gross. She batted her eyes, clutching her hands in front of her and releasing her shoulders so she looked like a balloon with a slow leak. "You'll be late to class, though."

Chip waved her off. "It's the least I can do to save the reputation of my school. I am a colonial hero, as you can see."

"You made a cracker!" I said. "It was probably by accident!"

They both ignored me.

"Please, fine madam, lead me to your polishing tools." Chip crooked one arm out toward Clover.

"Of course," she said sweetly. She snaked her hand through his arm, then gave me a glare. "As hall monitor, I'm afraid I must tell you to get to class, Thomas, or I'll have to write you up." She turned back to Chip and smiled again, and the two of them sashayed into the janitor's closet to find the polishing rags.

"Oh, brother," I mumbled as I started up the stairs.

2

I itched all through Biofeedback—my legs *keeping me from directing my energy toward an inward calm*, as my teacher Mrs. Breeze liked to say—and sagged all through Active Numbering. By the time I got to Four Square class—Pennybaker School's name for PE—I was ready to take off my spatterdashes, even if it meant having to do push-ups or pull-ups or getting my nose smashed by Buster Tallwell in football . . . again. I just wanted to be free from the pantyhose prison.

I had just gotten one leg out when I was shoved from

behind, knocking me into my locker. "Who are you supposed to be, nerd?"

Buster Tallwell's unique gift was feats of strength and extreme heightness. There was a rumor that Buster had already been scouted by the NBA and the NFL and the NHL and the FBI, but I think that last one was added just because people had already used up all the other letters and still wanted the rumor to sound important. But nobody could confirm any of it, because anyone who asked Buster Tallwell a question about his height mysteriously ended up duct-taped to the mats on the gym wall. Chip had been duct-taped five times. He even started carrying his own duct tape. He called it his Tallwell Tape, because Chip Mason was a good sport about everything.

Questions That Could Get You Tallwell-Taped to the Gym Wall, in No Particular Order

1. How's the weather up there?
2. Can you see my house from here?
3. Does it hurt when meteorites hit you in the head?
4. Do you have to duck when airplanes fly by?
5. Have you ever put a flashlight in your mouth and stood by the ocean on a stormy night?

6. Can I borrow your eraser? (Apparently Buster Tallwell wasn't a big fan of sharing, either.)

I shimmied out of my dress shirt, and my skin sighed with relief. I crammed it into my locker and pulled out my gym clothes, which hadn't been washed in sixty-six days, making me the current record-holder in the unofficial Pennybaker School Smelly Shirt Contest. Wesley had been ahead of me until parent-teacher conferences, when his mom pulled his yellow shirt out of his gym locker and screamed in disgust. Apparently it had been white when she'd sent it in at the beginning of the year.

"I asked you a question, nerd," Buster said, leaning over me menacingly, blocking out the light. **(7. Does your head get hot from light bulbs?)**

"Oh, this?" I asked, plucking the spatterdashes off the floor and dropping them in my locker. "Philadelphus Philadelphia."

"Who?"

"Philadelphus Philadelphia."

"You're making that up."

I shimmied into my shorts, my legs feeling wonderfully breezy and free. "Nope."

"Nobody is named Philawhatever."

"Well, maybe not anymore, but this guy sure was."

He rolled his eyes. "Let me guess. He had a brother named New Jersius New Jersey."

13

"No, he—"

"And a sister named Californius California. A whole family named after cities."

"Um, those are states, and—"

"Oh! I know another. Francius Francey."

"That's a country. And you added a Y."

"Fine. Australius Australia." .

"Continent."

He narrowed his eyes at me. "Are you saying I don't know what I'm talking about?"

I held my arms up in surrender. "No. I swear. I was just . . . His name was actually Jacob Meyer, but he went by Philadelphus Philadelphia. And, trust me, I think it's stupid, too. I just had to pick someone."

The truth was, I kind of related to Jacob Meyer. He was the first American-born magician. He was kind of a big deal, made a ton of money, performed for royalty across Europe, and even got banished from Prussia for freaking out the king. Freaking out kings sounded like a pretty cool skill to put on your job applications.

But, even better, Jacob Meyer, aka Philadelphus Philadelphia, used science in his magic. Specifically, he used alchemy, which Chip explained to me was mostly about trying to turn lead into gold. That sounded like exactly the reason I was at Pennybaker in the first place.

As much as I hated dressing up, learning about people

like Jacob Meyer was pretty cool. And Mr. Faboo, our Facts After the Fact teacher, was awesome at teaching us interesting stuff about regular people, because he believed regular people were just as important in history as wars and treaties, which made regular guys like me feel kind of important. Plus, he didn't believe in memorizing dates or taking tests, which made thirty days of suffocated calves totally worth it.

Buster continued. "You should have picked someone cool, like . . . like . . . like the guy who built Plymouth Rock."

I waited for him to say *Just kidding* or something, but he didn't. In fact, he seemed pretty pleased with himself for having had such a great idea. "It wasn't built," I said. "It's a rock."

"What are you saying? That I don't know about rock-building?" He leaned even farther over me. I was starting to understand why Chip spent so much time on the wall. There was no way he would be able to resist giving a lecture on the history of rock formation. He would probably even ask to go home so he could don his geology socks.

I, however, liked keeping my feet on the ground. "No, no, of course not, Buster. I think the Plymouth Rock thing is a really good idea. You should ask Mr. Faboo about it."

I wondered what Mr. Faboo would look like duct-taped to the gym wall.

"We're introducing a new unit today, fellas," Coach Abel said as we grunted and groaned over our calisthenics. "Don't quit, now; nobody told you to stop. Thirteen, fourteen, good . . ." He walked through our squad lines, every so often pausing to straighten someone's jumping-jack arms.

"Basketball?" Buster yelled. He was already done with his calisthenics. Buster Tallwell was born done with his calisthenics.

"Nope."

"Football?" Buckley Manor asked.

"Nope."

"Handball?" Colton Wood said between grunts.

"Nope."

"Cheerleading?" a voice asked. A very high, squeaky, non-boy voice. Samara Lee was standing just inside the gym door, her hands on her hips. Worse, the entire girls' Four Square class was standing behind her.

"Let me through, let me through." There was some scuttling around in the crowd of girls, and then Miss Allegro, the teeny music teacher and high school dance team coach, popped out. She was holding a clipboard in one hand and a portable stereo in the other. "We're here!" she announced in her teeny voice.

We all glanced at one another.

"Excellent!" Coach Abel clapped one time. "I was just getting ready to announce our new unit." He turned to us.

"Boys," he said, sweeping his arm out wide toward the girls, "meet your new unit."

Nobody moved. Nobody spoke. Nobody breathed. Not even Chip Mason, who never missed an opportunity to chime in on an awkward situation.

"Excuse me, Coach Abel, sir? I have a query-slash-declaration."

I was wrong. Of course Chip Mason was going to chime in.

Coach patted the air with his hands. "You can't have any questions yet. I haven't even told you what the unit is."

"Yes, but—"

"I think you fellas will like this unit. It's a cooperative effort."

"But—"

"It will give you a chance to get to know your fellow students better."

"Of course, but—"

"It will stretch your boundaries."

"But—"

"Take your learning to new heights."

"Sir—"

"Teach you to grow and—oh, what is it, Chip?"

Chip pushed his glasses up higher on his nose, then clasped his hands behind his back—his favorite lecturing posture—and paced in front of his squad line a few times.

Finally he stopped, looked at Coach Abel, and said, "You do realize those are girls."

We all nodded and mumbled in agreement.

"Sit down, Mr. Mason," Coach said. "Of course I realize they're girls. And that was not a question."

Chip held up one finger. "That's why I said query-slash-declaration. You see, a quer—"

Wesley elbowed Chip in the side of the knee. Chip lowered his finger, pushed his glasses up again, and pressed his lips together tightly.

Coach Abel continued. "As I was saying, these fine young ladies are going to be joining you for a while." All eyes, round and terrified, drifted over to the girls. "Miss Allegro has been kind enough to offer to teach the next unit, which will be . . . *dance*."

He said the last word really quickly. We traded confused glances.

"Did you say 'pants'?" Dawson Ethan asked.

"France. I think we're doing something French," Colton said.

"Ants?" someone asked from the back row.

"Ooh, finally! An entomology unit!" Chip said, bouncing a little on his toes.

"No, not 'ants,' you dummy. He said 'trance.' We're going to learn how to hypnotize people. I bet you could do it,

Thomas. *Woo woo . . .*" This from Julian Frood, who was wiggling his fingers at me.

"For the thousandth time, Julian," I said, "hypnosis is not magic, and I don't hypnotize people."

"Actually," Chip said, "magicians have used hypnosis for—"

"Dance!" a voice yelled, cutting off Chip and making us all jump. Patrice Pillow was standing in the middle of the crowd of girls, wearing her all-black gym uniform (complete with black beret), her arms crossed, a scowl on her face. "He said 'dance.' Not 'pants' or 'France' or 'ants' or 'trance.' *Dance*. And we're no happier about it than you are."

"I'm happy about it," Fiona Patada said. She did a quick spin and a curtsy.

"That's because you're a dancing genius," Wesley said. Fiona placed her hand over her heart and curtsied even lower. "Unlike the rest of us," Wesley added.

"Now, now," Miss Allegro said, walking briskly to the front of the gym. She placed the stereo on a cart and plugged it in. "You don't have to be a genius to dance. You just have to be willing."

"Well, that counts me out," I said, expecting everyone to laugh. But nobody did. They were all too worried about what would come next.

What they didn't know was that I was completely serious.

There's a saying that people who can't dance have two left feet. I was pretty sure I had two backward feet. In third grade, I got down and boogied at my cousin Peter's wedding reception—which meant I flailed around and hoped to stay upright. Only during the Chicken Dance, I didn't exactly stay upright. I flailed myself onto the ground, tripping the bride, who teetered into the groom, who lurched forward into his best man, who flung his dance partner into the cake, which splattered on the floor, causing Great-Aunt Ethel to slip and catch herself on the punch table, causing an avalanche of crashing glasses and pink, fizzy punch that ruined the bride's shoes. I had a serious Staring at Mom's Tonsils Because She Was Yelling So Hard Adventure all the way home, and I swore off dancing forever. Like, *forever* forever. Just thinking about dancing made my stomach gurgle.

Miss Allegro clapped her hands three times, her heels together and her posture so good that even Mom would have nothing to complain about. "Everyone up!"

Reluctantly, we all stood.

"Good. Now girls, come join the boys." The girls moved just as reluctantly as we had.

"What kind of dance are we doing, Miss Allegro?" my friend Flea asked. Flea only came up to the shoulder of even the shortest girl.

"Ballroom," she said triumphantly. "We will learn basics in class that you will use to choreograph your own routines.

And at the end of our unit, we will have a program to show your parents all you've learned. Isn't that exciting?"

About as exciting as pantyhose.

There was a lot of grumbling going on, until finally Coach Abel held up his hand to silence us. It kind of worked, but ballroom dance—*with girls*—was really a two-hand-silence kind of job.

"Miss Allegro and I will randomly select your partners. There will be no swapsies, no tradebacks, no refusals or returns. You get who you get, and we expect you all to be mature ladies and gentlemen about it. Let's make two lines. Boys over here, girls over here; face one another and count off."

Everyone shuffled around, confused and irritated, as we all tried to pair up with just the right person to avoid maximum humiliation. I planted my eyes firmly on Patrice Pillow, trailing the line and counting carefully so I could be assigned to dance with her.

There were many reasons to pair up with Patrice Pillow:

1. **She was the only person who'd believed in me when Helen Heirmauser's head went missing.**
2. **She was nice.**
3. **She had four brothers, so she wasn't afraid to sock you one if you made her mad. Because . . .**
4. **She was not girly.**

And, most important:

5. She definitely didn't want to do this any more than I did.

The lines eventually got settled, Coach Abel yelling at us to find our spots or he would find them for us, and I was thrilled to be standing directly across from Patrice. Coach began counting off, and, one by one, couples found practicing space on the gym floor.

He was only a dozen or so people away when Chip wriggled into line next to me.

"Hey, Thomas. Took me forever to find my dance socks in my locker. Well, technically they're square-dancing socks, but they'll do in a pinch until I find my ballroom dancing socks at home tonight."

"You have ballroom dancing socks?"

He nodded. "They're a little worn, but Mom can darn them."

"You have . . . Why? How did you wear out ballroom dancing socks? . . . You know what? Never mind. I don't want to know. You need to move, or I won't get to be with Patrice."

Coach was getting closer. Chip pushed up his glasses somberly. "It's supposed to be a random pairing. It can't be random if you position yourself to get a particular person."

"That doesn't matter. Just move."

"It very much matters, Thomas. You're not supposed to work the system to your advantage."

"Nobody cares," I hissed. "Just . . . switch places with me."

"I don't think I should."

I grabbed his shoulders and tried to maneuver him, but Chip could make himself extra heavy when he wanted to. "Go."

"No."

"Go."

"No. Oh, that tickles, Thomas." He giggled.

I tried to come up with a plan—maybe one of the girls down the line wouldn't mind moving up—but Coach was too fast for me.

"Eighteen," he said, touching the top of my head with the palm of his hand.

With his other hand, he pointed at Sissy Cork, who trudged forward, holding out her hand.

"Come on, you," she said angrily. Sissy Cork's unique talent was arm wrestling, and I had seen her make at least three boys cry. If anyone should've been paired up with Buster Tallwell, it was her. I was a little afraid of having her anywhere near my arms.

"I don't have all day, you know," she said. She walked in front of me through the gym until we found a spot. Sissy Cork and I had absolutely nothing in common.

I looked back at the line. Chip Mason was walking

proudly to an empty spot with Patrice's arm hooked through his. He caught my eye and brightened, giving me a wave.

I turned around and didn't wave back.

Forget the cracker guy. Chip should have been Benedict Arnold.

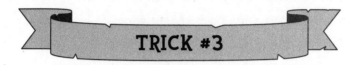

TRICK #3

A TEACHER APPEARS

I wasn't sure how somebody named Philadelphus Philadelphia would talk. Jacob Meyer was actually born in America, so while all my classmates were running around trying on their British and Scottish and German accents in preparation for Act After the Fact, I was pretty much just talking normally.

"Top o' the day to ya, laddy," Wesley said, coming up behind me as I walked to class. I knew Wesley's Irish accent well; it was one of his favorites. He was wearing a billowy pair of pants stuffed into knee-high boots. He had on a fancy-looking coat and a round hat with a feather sticking out of it.

"Hey, where are your pantyhose?" I asked, pointing to his legs.

"I believe you mean leggings," he said.

"Whatever. You're wearing pants."

He stopped, brought one arm across his chest, and tipped his chin up importantly. "That is because I am in character." His tone was lofty, his Irish accent gone.

"We're all in character. What gives?"

"I am a character within a character."

"Huh?"

He went slack and gave me a frustrated grunt. "I'm Lewis Hallam. I, along with my brother William, created the very first acting troupe in America. We opened with *The Merchant of Venice*. That's Shakespeare." Again with the arm across the chest, only this time Wesley bowed low. "I am in costume." He had now adopted an English accent. "Thus, I am playing a character who is playing a character." He straightened and grinned. "Pretty cool, huh?"

"Anything is cool if you don't have to wear pantyhose."

"Leggings," Dawson Ethan said as he passed by.

"Whatever," I said.

"Who do you think Mr. Faboo will be this year?" Owen asked, coming up on my other side. "Man, these things itch."

"Tell me about it. Who are you?"

"Thomas Godfrey, inventor of the octant."

"What's an octant?" Wesley and I said at the same time.

Owen pulled out an odd-looking triangular contraption. "It measures for navigation." He shrugged. "It's cool if you like gadgets."

Nobody liked gadgets more than Owen. He liked gadgets so much that he wore a metal spaghetti strainer on his head because he thought it gave him a better wireless signal.

"So who do you think Faboo will be?" Owen repeated.

"Benjamin Franklin?" I guessed.

"Not unknown."

"George Washington?"

"You're not even trying. Last year he was some guy who made a turtle submarine. Bushes somebody or other."

"David Bushnell," Flea said, joining us. "The year before that, he was Henry Knox, who was this really fat general who died from eating a chicken bone. Mr. Faboo carried a live chicken with him all day."

"To pay homage," Wesley said. He said "homage" like HO-MAWJ. "To the chicken, that is."

"Whoever he is, you know it'll be g—"

We rounded the corner into the classroom doorway and stopped, two other kids slamming into us from behind.

Mr. Faboo wasn't there. On his favorite day of the year. Act After the Fact Month was like Christmas to Mr. Faboo, and all he could talk about for the past three weeks was how excited he was to see everyone's costumes. He should have been standing in front of the classroom in an elaborate Revolutionary War getup. Instead, some bald guy with frizzy tufts of hair over his ears stood by the teacher's desk. He was wearing a suit. A brown suit. With a brown shirt. And a brown tie. Pennybaker brown. No wig. No spatterdashes. Not even a cravat.

"Come in, students," the sub said when he saw us jammed together in the doorway. He waved his hands. "Don't just stand there. You're a fire hazard."

"Who are you?" Owen asked.

"I am Mr. Smith. Now, come in or you'll all be tardy. I would hate to give a detention on my first day. Take a reading packet on the way to your seats."

Slowly we inched to our seats, each picking up a heavy packet of photocopied papers, everyone looking at everyone else with questions in their eyes. Mr. Faboo was definitely not a photocopied-papers kind of teacher. *Mr. Smith?* Flea mouthed to me. I shrugged.

"Excuse me, Mr. Smith?" Clara Willis said, waving and wiggling her hand high.

"Yes?" Mr. Smith already looked weary.

"Where is Mr. Faboo? Is he getting into his costume?"

"I'm afraid not," Mr. Smith said. "Mr. Faboo has taken a leave of absence."

"Leave of absence?" Patrice Pillow repeated. "You mean, like, gone for a long time?"

"Maybe forever," Mr. Smith said. We all gasped. "Now, if you'll pay attention to the first page of . . . Yes?"

Clara had raised her hand again. "Why?"

He pointed to the packet in front of him. "Because we're going to read from it."

"No, I mean, why isn't he coming back?"

Mr. Smith smooshed his lips together, making his brown mustache crunch up to his nose. "That, I'm afraid, I am not privileged to share with you. Now, if you—"

"Is he sick?" Clara asked, interrupting him.

"I don't think so. Page one—"

"Is he dead?" Patrice Pillow interjected, her pencil poised over her notebook. Patrice had been writing a horror novel since she was three. She was always looking for interesting corpses to add.

"No, of course n—"

The questions started coming fast and furious.

"Did he move away?"

"Get married?"

"Have a baby?"

"Is he in jail?"

"Is he on the run from police?"

"Did he get a better job?"

"Perhaps he is on sabbatical in someplace exciting and ancient, such as Ephesus or Teotihuacan, delving into the honorable pursuit of philology." This from Chip. Of course.

"Phil-what-ogy?" Clara asked.

"Philology. The study of the historical development of language. He being a history devotee, as it were."

"Teoblahblahtican sounds made up," Buckley said.

"No, it's a real place," Chip said. "It's in Mexico. Ephesus is in Turkey. Funny thing about Turkey: my mom put my Turkish socks into the dryer and—"

"I like turkey," Colton said. "Now I'm hungry."

"You already had Meat and Greet. You can't be that hun—"

"Enough!" Mr. Smith shouted, making us all jump. "Mr. Faboo is absent. He won't be back anytime soon. Probably not ever. Why is nobody's business but his. We are not discussing Turkey or socks or philology. Now, please direct your attention to page one. We are starting the Civil War."

More confused glances were exchanged.

"Um . . ." Clara had raised her hand again.

Mr. Smith seemed to wilt a little bit, trying to decide whether to call on her. "Yes," he said wearily. "What is it?"

"We're actually in the colonial period," she said. "Late sixteen hundreds to early eighteen hundreds. We have costumes." She gestured to the dress she was wearing.

"It's Act After the Fact Month," Wesley said. We all nodded.

"Not anymore," Mr. Smith said. He pointed to Owen, who was scratching his leg determinedly under his desk. "These costumes are a distraction. And they're silly. Tomorrow I want you all back in your regular uniforms."

"No pantyhose?" I asked, the words blurting out of me before I could stop them.

"They're leggings," half the class said in unison.

"Whatever," I mumbled.

"No to anything that isn't part of the usual Pennybaker School uniform," Mr. Smith said.

"Mr. Smith?" Clara again.

"Yes?" he said with a sigh.

"What's your unique gift?"

He narrowed his eyes and thought about it. "I suppose I don't have one, really. I'm just a regular teacher. And I'd like to teach now. Who wants to start reading aloud?"

Hugo Helmuth, whose unique gift was tightrope walking, raised his hand and began reading. But I didn't hear any of what he was saying; I was too busy concentrating on the fact that I wouldn't have to wear spatterdashes anymore, now that Mr. Smith had banned costumes.

No pantyhose.

No itchy legs.

Just regular history class, with a regular teacher.

Which meant Mr. Smith was normal—totally normal, in a crowd of the most non-normal people you could ever meet in your life. The kind of normal I'd been wishing for since I started attending Pennybaker School.

Absolutely, positively normal.

"Thomas Fallgrout?" I looked up. He was consulting a seating chart.

"Huh?"

"Not 'huh.' 'Yes, sir.' Understood?"

"Yeah."

He clenched his jaw. "Not 'yeah.' 'Yes, sir.'" He straightened his spine. "Listen up, class. The days of tomfoolery in this class are over. You will have respect. You will learn the material. You will read aloud when I ask you to read aloud. And you will pay attention so you know where to begin reading when I call on you. Is that understood, Mr. Fallgrout?"

I shifted in my seat, feeling the tops of my ears burn with embarrassment. "Uh, yeah. I mean, yes. Yes, sir."

"Start reading."

Yep, Mr. Smith was normal.

And kind of mean.

And I was pretty sure he wouldn't be teaching us about guys who died from chicken bones. Or about Jacob Meyer or John Pearson. Or about any regular guys who were important to history just by being part of it.

I missed Mr. Faboo already.

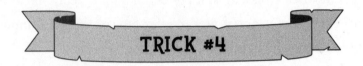

TRICK #4

THE HIDDEN GRANNY TRICK

"Well, that's it," I said, tossing my backpack onto the stairs as soon as I walked in the front door. "I have to quit school."

"Lucky for the school," my sister, Erma, said, bounding down the stairs and jumping over my backpack. She stuck her thumbs in her ears and wiggled her fingers at me as she passed. I was still waiting for Erma to get over her "immature phase," as Mom called it. So far, it seemed that this phase was going to last a long, long time. Maybe forever. Maybe I would be a professional dancer before Erma would be a mature anything.

Ever since Chip started going to Pennybaker School, Mom and Mrs. Mason took turns driving. Today was Mrs. Mason's turn, which meant I hadn't been able to take off my costume in the car. Instead, I took it off in the living room, where I had more privacy.

"What's going on now?" Mom asked, carrying an armload of empty soda cans tied to a thin rope. "Why do you have to quit school this time?"

When she put it that way, it seemed like maybe I threatened to quit school too much. I struggled to free my leg without falling over. Taking pantyhose off was no easier than putting them on. "One word," I said. "Dance." I finally got the leg loose and nearly fell over with relief. I bent to scratch every inch of my leg.

"I don't understand," Mom said.

"Dance. Our new unit in gym class is dance," I said. "And my partner is Sissy Cork, and she keeps looking at my skinny arms like she means business." I flexed, just to illustrate how puny my arm muscles were.

"Oh, Thomas, don't be dramatic. I'm sure it's not as bad as all that."

"It is."

She started up the stairs. "It's just a little dance."

"Remember Cousin Peter's wedding, Mom?"

She paused, grimaced, and then kept moving. "That was a long time ago."

"Still traumatic." I yanked my second leg free and followed her in my boxers and button-down shirt. "Did I mention it's ballroom dance?"

"Sounds like fun to me. An adventure!"

"*Couples* ballroom dance?"

"I'm sure it will be fine. Besides, Erma can teach you."

Erma, who was famous for always hanging around where she shouldn't be hanging around so she could hear what she shouldn't be hearing, popped out from under the stairs. "If you can teach a monkey sign language, I suppose it's possible to teach a monkey to dance," she said. She mimed scratching her armpits, ape-style.

"No way. The only thing worse than dancing with Sissy Cork is dancing with Erma." A Dancing Adventure was bad enough. A Dancing with Erma Adventure might make me actually die.

"Fraidycat," Erma said.

Mom gave Erma a pointed look and then turned back to me. "Really, Thomas, you will survive."

I followed her up the stairs. "But, Mom . . . can't you tell the coach I can't do it? Tell him I have too many toes. Or wobbly knees. Or an allergy to arm wrestlers." I faked a sneeze. "That one might be true."

"You just might like it. And you'll never know unless you try," she said. "Now, go pick up your costume. You have to wear it again tomorrow."

"No, I don't," I said.

"What? Why not? I'm not writing you a special note to get out of it, Thomas. We've been through this."

"You don't need to. Mr. Faboo is gone, and we have the meanest substitute ever, and he said no more costumes. And

36

then he gave us homework. Which is another reason why I have to quit."

"Homework won't kill you. And I would think it would make you happy not to have to wear a costume, with all the complaining you've been doing about it."

I thought about it. Technically, she was right. It just felt wrong. "I guess." I started to walk away. Mom got to Grandma Jo's room and stood up on her tiptoes, attaching the soda-can rope to the door frame with a pushpin. "What are you doing?"

"Huh? Oh." She drove another pushpin into the rope a little farther down, and then another. "I'm booby-trapping your grandmother's door."

"Why?"

Mom let the string of cans hang loose. She turned to me and blew a strand of hair out of her face. "Because she's not getting into trouble."

"Do you mean she *is* getting into trouble?"

"Nope. She's *not* getting into trouble."

"Ooo-kaaay. Isn't that a good thing?"

"Not when it's your grandmother. I just know she's hiding something from me. Sneaking out. Or sneaking in. Or just . . . sneaking."

Mom had a point. Grandma Jo was definitely not the sit-at-home-and-knit-blankets kind of grandmother. She was more the jump-from-one-rooftop-to-another-with-someone-named-Barf kind of grandmother. Grandma Jo crashed her motorcycle once and broke a couple of bones, and Mom freaked out and made her move in with us so she could keep her from getting hurt. Grandma Jo didn't mind getting hurt, though. She thought danger was the exciting part of life. So Mom was probably right—if Grandma Jo wasn't doing anything dangerous, she was definitely hiding something.

I went downstairs and picked up my clothes, then found Grandma Jo sitting in front of the television, a game of solitaire set up on the TV tray in front of her.

"You okay?" I asked.

She blinked at me. The TV screen reflected off the lenses of her glasses. "What?"

"Is something wrong?"

"I'm perfectly fine. Why do you ask, Thomas?"

"When was the last time you went to the skate park?"

She flipped a card over and placed it on top of another one. "Oh, it's been a while, I suppose."

"What about parkour? The jumping off really high things onto other really high things?" I used my fingers to mimic someone running and jumping, the way Grandma Jo always did when she talked about it.

She scrunched up her face and rubbed her knee. "Too much bouncing for this old body."

I narrowed my eyes at her. "How's the skydiving these days?"

She placed another card. "I wouldn't know."

"Rodeo clowning?"

"Nope."

"Motorcycle racing?"

"Nuh-uh."

We were silent for a moment, our eyes locked. "I don't believe you," I said.

She put down the card she was holding and scooted the tray out of the way, then patted the sofa next to her. "Sit, Thomas." I did. "There comes a time in a granny's life when she needs to slow down," she said, snaking her arm around me. She smelled like mints and motor oil. Pretty typical for Grandma Jo. "Your mother doesn't like it when I do danger-ous things, so I'm ready to give it all up—to just be a granny and watch your sister dance and watch you do . . . whatever it is you're doing in your mother's pantyhose."

"They're leggings," I muttered. "And they're mine, not Mom's."

"And your magic," she said brightly. "I'll get to watch you do your magic. I miss magic. It'll be like having Rudy around again."

Rudy was my grandpa, and he was a magician. When he died, Grandma Jo gave his magic trunk to me because she knew how much I liked watching him perform. In the bottom of his trunk, I'd found a bunch of chemicals and instruc-tions on how to use those chemicals to perform science tricks. Sort of like Philadelphus Philadelphia and his alchemy.

Grandpa Rudy's magic trunk was what had landed me at Pennybaker School, after I turned some pennies silver. It was just a reaction between copper, zinc, and sodium hydroxide, but Mom was convinced I was a genius and sent me off to be with other geniuses. So when it came down to it, this whole dancing situation was Grandpa Rudy's fault.

"It's just time for me to focus on being a granny, Thomas," Grandma Jo said. She started pulling the TV tray back in front of her. Two cards fell off. I bent down to pick them up for her. "Besides, there are some really great shows on TV nowadays. Today I learned how to bake pumpkin pull-apart bread and get bloodstains out of carpet. Of course, only one of those will be handy for me to know." She smiled, patted me on the head, and went back to her game.

It wasn't until I was all the way upstairs and hanging up my costume that I realized she had never specified which one.

TRICK #5

LOADED LEVITATION

I still wasn't sure if I was on Team Mom or Team Grandma Jo, but my conversation with Grandma Jo had reminded me of something. After I hung up my clothes, I dropped to my knees and pulled Grandpa Rudy's old trunk out from under my bed.

I opened it and found Bill's food dish. Bill was Grandpa Rudy's rabbit. One day, Grandpa Rudy put Bill in a hat, and he never came out again. We suspected he had hopped away during the show, but Grandpa Rudy could never let his dish go, just in case Bill was in another dimension and would return wanting dinner. I guess traveling between dimensions could make a rabbit pretty hungry.

I pawed through the trunk, carefully setting aside the carnival bottles and linking rings and the coin you could bite right through, and finally found the tiny reporter's notebook that Grandpa Rudy had filled with lists of tricks. I remembered all of them, down to the very last breakaway fan. I ran my finger down the list until I found what I was looking for.

"Levitation," I whispered, tapping the paper.

According to Grandpa Rudy's chicken scratch, levitation was one of his easiest tricks, and he could do it a bunch of ways. He could make his assistant, Irene, float above a table. He could make a pencil lift out of someone's pocket and drift to his hand. And he could even make himself levitate while standing up.

In other words, he could make it look like he was hovering in the air, like a leaf. Or a feather. Or . . . a dancer.

It was a long shot. Sissy wasn't a genius, but she was probably close enough to know the difference between hovering and dancing.

Still, it was worth a try. If Chip and I could pull off the greatest disappearing-head trick of all time, like we'd done with the Heirmauser head, I could pull off a floating-dance trick.

Besides, whenever Grandpa Rudy did the levitation thing, it seriously weirded people out. And if I couldn't get people to believe I was dancing, I could distract them long enough not to have to do it. Maybe if I rolled my eyes around in my head and let my tongue hang out and a little bit of drool drop down, people would get scared enough that Coach Abel would have to cancel the dancing unit altogether.

Yep. Definitely worth a try.

2

I worked on levitating until Mom called me down for dinner.

"What on earth were you doing up there?" she asked when I got to the kitchen.

"Hey, pal," Dad said at the same time. He'd just gotten home from work and hadn't changed out of his work clothes yet.

"Hey, Dad," I said, rubbing my elbow. "Sorry, Mom, I was working on something."

"You were crashing around like a scared buffalo," Erma said, scooting in her chair. "Crash, boom, *mooo.*"

"Sounds exciting," Grandma Jo said. She scooped a big spoonful of corn onto her plate.

Erma giggled. "Scared buffalos aren't exciting."

"They are if you're in their way," Grandma Jo said. I avoided her eyes. I was the only one in the family who knew that Grandma Jo had a hobby that involved being in the way of big animals.

Mom pointed at Grandma Jo with a spatula. "Aha! I knew it! You've been scaring buffalo!"

"Are you even listening to yourself right now?" Grandma Jo said. "Where would I get a buffalo around here?"

43

Mom thought about it, chewing her lip, then lowered the spatula back down onto the platter of burgers. "I suppose," she murmured. "But if anyone could . . ."

"What were you working on, pal?" Dad asked, trying to change the subject.

"Oh, just doing some magic." I said it lightly, the way you would say *Oh, just watching TV* or *Oh, just taking a shower* or *Oh, just having a snack.*

"What kind of magic?" Dad asked.

"Blowing things up, probably," Erma said.

"Eat your burger, Erma," I said.

"Make me."

"Stop it, you two," Mom said. "Blowing things up isn't magic."

Sometimes it is, I wanted to say, but I figured saying that to Mom wouldn't be in my best interest. As it was, Mom was always worrying about things that could possibly happen.

Things That Could Possibly Happen, by Thomas Fallgrout's Mom

1. You could break your leg.
2. You could break your neck.
3. You could break your leg *and* your neck if you don't get off that thing right now, and I mean it, young man.

4. You could knock your eyeball out with pretty much anything.
5. You could make the whole family a laughingstock with a stunt like that.
6. You could regret that you even thought about it, mister.
7. You could get sick, and who would put their mouth on something like that, anyway?
8. You could set your hair on fire. (To be fair, she was right about this one. We don't really talk about it anymore.)
9. You could bust your head wide open, so both of you put down those rocks.
10. Your face could get stuck that way. (Hint: it is never a good way.)

"Blowing things up can be pretty magical," Grandma Jo said.

"Aha!" Mom cried, pointing with the spatula again. "What have you been blowing up?"

Grandma Jo held her burger like a shield. "Down, woman. I haven't blown up anything more than a baked potato in the microwave." She leaned toward me and winked. "It was awesome," she whispered. "Spud guts everywhere."

"That's it," Mom said, tossing down the spatula. It rattled on the plate, then flopped off and clattered to the floor. "I don't know what you're up to"—she pointed at Grandma Jo, with her finger this time—"or what *you're* up to"—she pointed at me—"but it stops this instant."

"I'm not doing anything!" Grandma Jo and I said at the same time.

Mom huffed. She scooted in her chair, primly spreading a napkin on her lap. She got settled, took a deep breath, and picked up her burger. "So. What did you do today?" she asked Dad.

He chewed and swallowed, looking very thoughtful, then ran his tongue over his teeth and said, "When I was a kid, we used to blow up dog poop with firecrackers."

"Cool!" Erma, Grandma Jo, and I all said.

Mom grunted and bit into her burger angrily.

We ate in silence after that. I imagined Dad, Grandma Jo, and I were all thinking about the same thing—the awesomeness of blowing up dog poop. Erma, meanwhile, was humming and swinging her feet. Mom was chewing her food like she expected it to fight back. They all forgot to ask again what I'd been doing upstairs. Which was a good thing. I was pretty sure nobody would understand why I wanted to float out of ballroom dancing.

"May I be excused?" I asked when I was finished.

"Sure, pal," Dad said. "Got homework?"

"He's got to dance," Erma said. She giggled and pantomimed monkey gestures again.

I scooted away from the table and took my plate to the sink.

"Thomas, let your sister help you," Mom said.

"Mom—"

"I'm not asking," she said.

She didn't need to finish the sentence.

11. You could push Mom to say, "I'm not asking; I'm telling," and then she would yell at you so hard your eyelashes would blow off.

~

"So what song are you dancing to?" Erma asked, coming into the living room where I was trying to do some math homework.

"I'm not," I said, not looking up.

"You get to choose your own?"

"No."

"Come on, Thomas." She stood in front of me, her arms out as if to dance.

"I don't want to," I said.

"I know that. But you can't dance on your sit bones. Get up."

"No."

"Mom said."

"I'm doing homework."

"I'm telling."

"Fine." I tossed my pencil onto my math book and stood up. No better time than the present to try out my new trick. I turned my body forty-five degrees away from Erma, straightened my left leg, and started to rise onto the toes of my right foot. "Oh. Wait. Uh-oh. I feel . . . I feel funny . . . I feel . . . like flying . . ." Slowly, I lifted into levitation. "Oh no! This isn't right! People don't float! Run away, Erma! Run! Before it happens to you!"

Erma rolled her eyes and kicked the back of my right knee, causing it to buckle and me to fall.

"Ugh. Grow up," she said.

She tossed her hair over her shoulder and flounced upstairs, leaving me on the floor, rubbing the back of my knee. At least I got out of dancing.

But maybe levitation wasn't the answer.

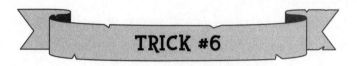

TRICK #6

POOF! POPULARITY!

The first thing I noticed when I woke up the next day was that I was freezing. I had wrapped my covers around me so tightly that I had a moment of panic, thinking I wouldn't be able to get out of them without help. But I thrashed around until I was loose, and then found the source of the chill.

The window was cracked open.

Had I done that? I didn't remember doing it. I had been really busy trying to perfect Grandpa Rudy's broken-arm trick.

I got up and shut the window, then got dressed.

When I got to school, there was a whole crowd on the front lawn. Maybe there was news about Mr. Faboo. Maybe he had come back and was demonstrating how to make a rope or skin a bear or something. I jumped out of Mom's car and headed straight over to find out what was going on.

No Mr. Faboo.

Instead, arms and legs and hands were flailing everywhere, and people were making weird noises and standing on one foot and counting. It was like they were all possessed. I was really creeped out until I saw the middle of the crowd and realized who was leading this nonsense.

"Chip," I said, pushing past Abigail Thew and her dance partner, Flea, who was at least a foot shorter than she was. "Where were you this morning? We stopped to pick you up."

"Oh, hi, Thomas," Chip said. He twisted his body this way and that, and then snapped back into place, doing something weird with his arms. "I'm instructing. Have you come to join the class?"

I spun around. Everyone was busy trying to twist their bodies into the same shape that Chip's had been in. Some of them were humming. "What class?"

"Dance class, of course. I found my ballroom dancing socks, and my instruction socks. I'm double-layered." He held a leg up in front of me. I pushed it back down. "It's a fine, chilly morning to be double-layered, don't you think?"

I remembered my window being open that morning. "It's cold."

"Dance will warm you. Join us. We're about to work on

our dégagés." He did something funny with his leg that looked like a cross between an ostrich stepping over a groundhog and Chip stepping onto a pile of garbage.

My stomach twisted disagreeably with wedding memories. "No, thanks. I'm not dancing," I said.

Chip stopped and stared at me, wide-eyed. "You have to. It's for an assignment."

"I'll take the F," I said.

"What about Sissy?" he asked. "If you get an F, so will she."

I had already thought about that and had a brilliant plan. "They'll get her another partner. They'll have to, because I think I broke my arm." I carefully placed my palm on the ground while surreptitiously sliding a plastic cup into my other armpit, then began spinning my hand around. Slowly, the crowd stopped moving and leaned in to see what I was doing. Perfect timing. I squeezed the cup, making a crunching sound. A girl squealed and fell backward into her dance partner's arms.

I moaned, rolled onto my back, and held my shoulder. "Oh. Ow. Ouch. Oh. Oh. Ooooh."

Chip began laughing, his glasses sliding down on his nose. "You're so funny, Thomas."

I glared. "I'm not funny. I broke my arm. Didn't you hear it? It was an awful crunching sound. I can't dance with a broken arm."

Chip laughed harder. "That's a really good trick, Thomas. You're getting better every day. Imagine if you borrowed my magic socks."

I stood up and angrily brushed off my knees. "I don't need your magic socks," I said. "And I'm not dancing with you. I have to polish the head of horror anyway."

"I already did."

"What do you mean you already did?"

"He got here early so he could help us," Owen said. He had a tablet on his lap and was busy tapping in notes about pirouettes and chassés, whatever those were. "And he had extra time, so he shined the bust already."

"But that's my job. They gave it to me. The hero."

"You're welcome, Thomas," Chip said, even though I definitely had not thanked him. "Anything to help a friend."

"He's really great like that," Wesley added in a cartoon tiger voice, stretching out the R in "great."

"Yeah. He's so great," I said sourly. I didn't know why exactly, but Chip's quick rise to stardom at Pennybaker was kind of bugging me. We were all uniquely gifted at something, but he seemed to be gifted at everything—including friend stealing and job stealing. "I'm going to go and . . ." I trailed off as I pushed through the crowd, mostly because I had no idea what I was going to go and do. All my best friends were busy dancing, and both my levitation and broken-arm tricks had failed. The bust had been polished. And it was too early to go to class.

I was just about to pull open the front door when a movement behind the bushes caught my eye. I let my hand fall away from the door handle and bent to get a look. I was pretty sure I knew what was moving around inside.

"Reap?"

"Hey, Thomas."

I scooted so that my back was against the wall and crouched down. "I thought Harriett moved away."

Harriett was a mother hedgehog Reap had been feeding. As soon as her babies were big enough, they had moved on.

"She did. There's something new under here. It's a baby."

I crouched lower, ducking my head to see under the bush where Reap was tossing bread crumbs. All I could see was a pair of eyes, which looked like two shiny black beads.

"What is it?"

"I don't know," Reap said. "I can't get it to come out. I've been trying for days. I've spoken to it in every language I know, and it doesn't answer." Reap's unique gift was hanging out with, talking to, and just generally being friends with animals. But he kept that a secret, because his entire family's unique gift was taxidermy, and he didn't want his animal friends to find out.

I grabbed a slice of bread and started ripping and tossing, too. The bread piled up. The eyes never moved.

"What if it's dangerous?" I asked, whispering, because that seemed like the right thing to do when you were within bread-tossing distance from something that might be dangerous.

Reap shrugged. "I guess I'll be in big trouble, then."

"What if it jumps out of the bush and chews your face right off?"

(Things That Could Happen **12. You could have your face chewed off by that stray. And then you could get rabies**.)

Reap laughed. "It wouldn't do that." But when he laughed, the animal startled. There was movement inside the bush, and the beady eyes were gone.

"Darn it," Reap said softly. He closed the bag of bread

and stood up. "Hey, Chip!" he called, waving over the bushes. "Thanks for getting the bread." He paused, listening. "Nope, not today. Maybe tomorrow." He turned toward me. "Man, Chip is such a great guy," he said. He sidestepped past me and made his way to the front door just in time for the warning bell to ring.

"Yeah. Really great," I said, remembering when I was the only one at Pennybaker who knew Reap's secret spot behind the bushes. And the only one at Pennybaker who knew Chip. "Everybody loves him. He must be wearing his popularity socks."

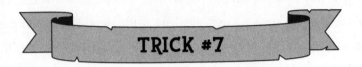

TRICK #7

THE FRIEND FORCE

"I kind of miss my costume," Wesley said as we walked into school after the warning bell rang.

"But you're always wearing a costume of some kind. I'm not sure if I've ever seen you in normal clothes."

He beamed. "Aw, thanks, buddy. That makes me feel a lot better."

Actors can be weird sometimes.

"Don't you wonder a little bit where Mr. Faboo might be?"

"Yeah," I said. "But I'm sure he'll be back. Maybe he just needed a break. This is a crazy school, after all."

Wesley stopped and looked at me with his eyebrows pushed together. "How so?"

"You mean you don't notice . . . You think this is . . . Never mind. I just mean school in general is crazy."

"Yeah, but it's not like Mr. Faboo to be gone. Ever."

"Maybe he took a vacation to somewhere historical. Like Boston. Or Egypt."

Wesley shook his head forcefully as I pulled open the big metal door for him. "Not during Act After the Fact Month. No way. Something is wrong. I can feel it *in my bones*." He gave a dramatic shiver, saying the last part in the kind of frightened voice you might hear in a scary movie.

I didn't want to say anything, but I could kind of feel it in my bones, too. Something was weird about the way the sub had acted. Like he owned the place. Like he was in charge forever. Like we were going to have to memorize dates and take tests and read things from photocopied packets.

I wasn't the biggest fan of Pennybaker's uniqueness. I wasn't the biggest fan of scary head statues or a principal who pantomimed, and I definitely wasn't the biggest fan of costumes. But I had become Mr. Faboo's fan, and I didn't want to think about what would happen if it was true that he was gone forever.

We walked into the vestibule, and the first thing I saw was Miss Munch, hands on hips, beaming as she admired Chip's polishing job.

I let my backpack drop to the floor and marched over.

"Oh, hello, Thomas," Chip said. "I was just showing Miss Munch the new polishing paste I've concocted for the

esteemed artwork in our fine school. Here, want a taste?" He held up a plastic bowl full of mucky white gunk. I jumped back.

"Gross! No."

"Suit yourself," he said. He leaned over and took a lick, then smacked his lips. "It's simply flour, salt, and vinegar. Nothing that can harm you. Some say that vinegar has been around since as far back as five thousand BC. Can you imagine? They even used it to clean wounds. Do you have any wounds, Thomas? I'm certain I'll have some paste left over."

"That's *my* statue," I said, crossing my arms. I knew I looked like a baby standing there, but I couldn't help it. *I* was the Helen Heirmauser Head Hero. *I* was the one who got to polish her every day. Sure, I forgot to do it a lot. And, sure, I complained a super lot. But still.

"Now, Thomas," Miss Munch said, placing her hand on my back, "Chip is only trying to help. Look how wonderfully his paste is working. Why, I haven't seen Helen's forehead shine so much since the heat wave of 1992."

"But that's my job. I'm the one who gets to shine her forehead." I couldn't believe those words had just come out of my mouth.

"Oh, here, Thomas. You can shine her tomorrow. I don't mind." Chip held out the rag he was using. It stunk like Easter eggs. He leaned in and whispered, "I've nibbled it only a little."

I held the rag between my thumb and forefinger, totally grossed out. "Thanks, I . . ." I leaned in closer. "I . . ." I leaned in closer still. "Hey! What happened to my name?"

He tapped his chin. "You know, I've been thinking about that for some time now, so I'm glad you brought it up. Thomas, of course, means 'twin.' That's easy. But Fallgrout is a bit of an enigma. It's not really Faulkner, which would have Scottish origins meaning Falconer, as in one who trains predatory birds. But it's not really Fa—"

"No, I mean my name on the statue." I pointed to the slightly lighter spot where a nameplate had been, bearing my name as the hero and rescuer of the Heirmauser memory. "You polished my name off!"

Chip leaned in closely and examined the bare spot over the top of his glasses. "Huh," he said. "I didn't notice. It must have fallen." He glanced around the floor, looking for it. "Maybe Mr. Crumbs swept it up. I'm sorry, Thomas. It was an accident."

I poked my finger into his chest. "It was not. You did it on purpose. Just like you stole my job on purpose, and started teaching dance on purpose, and—"

The bell rang, and everyone started scurrying toward their classrooms. Including Chip.

"I wasn't finished yelling at you," I called after him.

He turned, came back to me, smiled, and patted my arm. "Don't worry, Thomas. You'll have lots of yelling-at-me time later. Maybe at tomorrow morning's dance practice? Everyone will be there."

He walked briskly into the crowd and was soon swept away.

"Never!" I called toward his back, my stomach clenching at the word "dance" again. Wesley, Flea, and Owen wandered by. "Hey, you guys aren't going to do that stupid dancing thing in the morning, are you?" I asked, rolling my eyes.

"Well, uh . . ." Flea said, looking over his shoulder.

"We were," Owen said. "You should, too, Thomas. It's not so bad."

Just like pantyhose weren't so bad and bow ties weren't so bad and penny loafers with shiny pennies in the toes to look cute weren't so bad. All those things were bad! I would bet that Mom would call the dance a Ballroom Dance Adventure. And you knew that when Mom put the word "adventure" after something, it was bad.

They started to walk away. I caught Wesley by the sleeve.

"Dude," I said, trying to convey the rest of the sentence with my eyebrows.

Eyebrow Conversation 101

- The single raised eyebrow: What are you
  doing, dude?

- The double raised eyebrow: I can't believe you did that, dude.
- The double raised eyebrow with head tilted to one side: You better be with me on this, dude.
- The frowning eyebrows: Fine, have it your way, dude.

I went through all the eyebrow configurations with Wesley. He responded with his own addition:

- The raised and bunched-together eyebrows: Sorry, dude.

Wesley drifted away with the others, and I was left alone in the vestibule, staring at the faded spot where my name used to be.

Mr. Smith was writing a bunch of packet page numbers on Mr. Faboo's vintage blackboard when I got to class that afternoon. Mr. Faboo always used a piece of chalk with a quill taped to one end to write on the blackboard, but Mr. Smith was using a plain old piece of chalk. The quill was nowhere in sight. My heart sank. I liked the quill. It made history seem more alive, somehow. And I'd never seen Mr. Faboo without it. If it was gone, maybe he really was, too.

Wesley, Flea, Owen, and Chip were already seated. I was still kind of irritated about the dance lessons, so I tried to act like I didn't notice and instead sat in the front row, making Tabitha Rattlebag pause when she came into the room. Tabitha Rattlebag earned the top score in all her classes, and always had, ever since the day she was born. She probably cried the best in the hospital nursery. Tabitha Rattlebag always sat front and center.

Tabitha Rattlebag was just going to have to deal with it.

She harrumphed and sat behind me.

"Homework," Mr. Smith announced, putting down the chalk and brushing off his hands.

There was silence in the room, and then Clara spoke up. "You mean we're supposed to just, like, read it?"

Mr. Smith nodded.

"We're not supposed to make a rap song out of it?" Patrice Pillow asked.

"No; why would I have you do that?"

"A poem, maybe?" Samara Lee interjected. "Or a one-act play?"

"No, just read it and be ready for a quiz tomorrow."

"A quiz?" Buckley was incredulous.

"Yes. Ten points is all. Just over tonight's reading."

"A quiz," Buckley said again.

"Yes, Mr. Manor, a quiz." Mr. Smith was getting irritated. Again.

"It's just that we've never taken a quiz in this class before," Clara said.

"Or a test," Tabitha added sourly. "In my opinion, it's about time."

Mr. Smith was taken aback. "No quizzes? How does Mr. Faboo know whether you understand the lessons?"

"Role-play, mostly," I said. "Sometimes with costumes."

"Costumes are silly and a distraction," Mr. Smith said again. "We'll have no more of that in this class. From here on out, we read the material, discuss it in class—in an appropriate manner—and take tests to make sure everyone understands. Now, open your packets to the final page."

There was a lot of unhappy mumbling as people tugged their packets out of their backpacks—the ones who hadn't used theirs to make paper airplanes or save a trapped bug or play trash-can basketball, that is.

I felt a poke in my back. Wesley was giving me an eyebrow look.

- Eyebrows lifted and lips pooched together: You still think Mr. Faboo might come back, dude?

"Come on, Mr. Fallgrout, the class is waiting."

I opened my packet and spread it out on my desk.

Mr. Faboo was going to come back, even if I had to find him and haul him back to Pennybaker myself.

2

I waited outside the office bathroom for Principal Rooster. He came through the door, humming the Pennybaker alma mater, and almost ran into me. He jumped back. "Oh! Thomas. You startled me. You know students aren't allowed to use the office bathroom, right?"

"I need to talk to Mr. Faboo," I said.

"What?"

"It's about . . . It's about my costume. I'm not sure if Philadelphus Philadelphia would have worn white stockings or another color. Maybe blue. Or red. His name sounds pretty patriotic. I can buy another color. I like shopping for pantyhose." Sometimes, when my brain accidentally lets my mouth off its leash, my mouth hops over the fence and runs all around the neighborhood before I can catch it. I blushed. "I mean, I want to make sure I get an A on the Act After the Fact assignment, so I just need to make sure my panty—leggings are right. That's all." I flicked some imaginary lint off my shirt, trying to look bored.

Principal Rooster squinted at me. "I thought Mr. Smith canceled Act After the Fact."

"Yeah, but Mr. Faboo will probably want to do it when

he gets back. This gives me lots of time to shop." Seriously, mouth. Get back on the leash.

"Son." Principal Rooster placed his hand on my shoulder. When guys like Principal Rooster start looking deep into your eyes and calling you "son," you know it's bad news. "I think you can just let Act After the Fact go. Mr. Smith is going to be around for a while."

I swallowed. "For how long?"

"For . . ." He searched the ceiling as if trying to recall a specific date, then locked his eyes on mine again. "Ever."

Nope. I refused to accept that we would have quizzes and reading packets forever. No wigs, no quill chalk, no live chickens? Just plain old history? That sounded terrible.

The warning bell rang. "You should probably get to class now," Principal Rooster said. "You're going to be tardy."

I felt my whole body slump as I trudged away from his office. But then I had an idea. I sauntered over to Miss Munch's desk and went back to flicking imaginary lint. "So, I'm supposed to get Mr. Faboo's phone number from you," I said.

"Huh?"

I rolled my eyes dramatically and flapped my hand in Principal Rooster's direction. "Principal Rooster wants me to call him about something."

"I don't think so," she said.

"I already have it somewhere," I tried. "It would just be a lot easier on me if I didn't have to search for it." I fake yawned.

"Not happening," she said.

"I mean, I know it has a five in it." A bluff, but chances were pretty high that I was right—especially since everyone in town had a phone number that started with 815.

"Go to class, Thomas," Miss Munch said, going back to her paperwork.

"Fine," I mumbled, and turned to go.

"And, Thomas?"

I turned back to her hopefully.

"He's not coming back. So you should probably give up trying to find him."

I frowned. Give up? No way.

I was just getting started.

7

Chip didn't show up right away after school let out. I tried to get Mom to leave without him, but she swore she could see him kneeling in front of the Heirmauser statue with all the other students, and figured he would be right out.

"You really should spend more time doing that," she said to me as we watched through the car window.

"Why?"

"Because . . . people liked her."

"I didn't even know her. And she doesn't really look like

someone I would like." Little did Mom know how much I agreed with her. I should have been spending more time with the statue. Because it was my job.

Chip tumbled out of the school, pushed along by a tide of laughing friends. They were having the time of their lives. With *Chip Mason*. I wondered if they had ever seen him sing opera into a slice of pizza. Or woken up with him crouching on their windowsill watching them sleep.

No, for real. He really did that.

"Thank you for waiting for me, Mrs. Fallgrout," Chip said as he climbed into Mom's car.

"You're always welcome, Chip," Mom said. "We aren't in any sort of hurry, are we, Thomas?"

I clenched my teeth. I wasn't going to say anything to the statue-polishing nameplate thief. For all I cared, he could talk to the back of my head.

"Thomas?" Mom prompted. I still said nothing. "Thomas, why are you being rude?"

"Don't worry, Mrs. Fallgrout," Chip said. "He's probably just working on his ballroom dance in his head. We all are."

"Do you like to dance, Chip?" Mom asked, and for the whole ride home, I got to hear all about some guy named Vaslav Nijinsky, who was arguably the best male dancer of the twentieth century. And then I got to hear about Chip's assortment of dancing socks. He had one pair for every type of dance—and two for polka, because polka dancing made his feet extra sweaty.

When we finally got home, Mom pulled into the driveway and paused so Chip could get out. I stared straight ahead, unmoving.

"Are you going with him?" Mom finally asked.

"No," I said. "I have a magic trick to work on."

Mom looked skeptical, and I didn't blame her. Normally I would take off with Chip and we would plan our afternoon activities, which might include riding our bikes or hanging out by the creek or eating cheese and crackers on his front porch.

Ever since Chip and I became friends, after-school time got a lot more interesting and fun.

But today I was mad at him. And, okay, fine, I was kind of hurt, too. Wesley and the guys were my friends first. It was one thing to be friends. It was another to steal someone's life. He was stealing mine.

And, worse, he was doing it without me.

"I found it." Chip's fist slithered over the seat and opened up, something shiny resting on the palm. It was my nameplate. "I searched all through the dirt Byron had swept up. I even shined it a little. Watch." He angled the metal plaque until the sunlight caught it and bounced a beam right into my eyes. "Direct hit, human," he said in a robotic voice. "You are now my pet." We both cracked up as he dropped the tag into my lap. "Sorry I stole your job. I was just trying to help you out."

And that was why it was hard to stay mad at Chip for very long. And probably why everybody at Pennybaker already loved him.

"It's okay, Chip. No hard feelings."

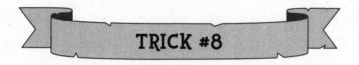

TRICK #8

SLEIGHT OF SISTER

After dinner, I locked myself in my room to work on my newest plan for getting out of dancing with Sissy Cork: a smoke screen.

I pulled out Grandpa Rudy's trunk and opened it. Inside were smoke cartridges. Ten of them, to be exact. I'd never used one before, mostly because I was a little bit afraid to. Grandpa Rudy didn't use them often, and I didn't have a great idea of how they were supposed to work.

I turned the package of cartridges over. The instructions were old and kind of worn off, but I knew the basics of using a smoke cartridge to make it look like your hand was smoking so something could disappear in a *poof* of smoke. Which was kind of cool. Especially since disappearing was exactly what I wanted to do.

If I could make a coin disappear in a *poof* with one

cartridge, maybe I could make myself disappear with ten. And if I did it at just the right time—say, right before we started our dumb dance, for instance—maybe it would cause enough of a distraction to give me time to get out of the gym.

I was still trying to read the instructions when Erma bounded through my door. I dropped the package and winced, half expecting the *poof* of smoke to happen right there in my bedroom.

"Jeez, Erma, haven't you ever heard of knocking?" I picked up the packet. "I'm busy."

She ignored me. "I have good news!" she said.

"The circus accepted your application and you're leaving tomorrow?"

"Very funny, but no." She hopped onto my bed and began jumping up and down—something she knew I hated, because it made my blankets all rumply and because it made Mom mad, and I always got yelled at for the things Erma did that made Mom mad. Especially when they happened in my territory. Mom never believed that Erma could be a diabolical infiltrator.

"Stop it."

She ignored me. "I'm going to your schoo-ool," she sang as she continued to jump.

I dropped the smoke cartridge package again. "What?"

"Mom talked to the coach and told her that I've been

dancing my whole life, and the coach wants me to come in and help teach a class. I'll be helping the students who are struggling. And one of those students is you! Isn't that cool?"

No. That was not cool. That was so opposite of cool, there wasn't even a word for it. It was like uncool with thirty-five "un"s in front of it. Erma teaching me to dance? Uncool. Erma teaching me to dance in my own school, in front of all the guys and the girls?

Horrifying.

"No way."

"Yep. I start tomorrow." She squealed a little and jumped higher.

"No way. Mom!" I hollered, stuffing the smoke cartridges back into the trunk and slamming it shut. Suddenly, figuring out a way to escape dancing just got a lot harder.

"She's busy," Erma said.

"Busy doing what?"

"I don't know. She and Dad are cutting branches off the oak tree."

Why would they be cutting branches off the oak tree? "You mean the tree right outside Grandma Jo's window?"

"Yep."

Oh. So that was why. Mom was afraid Grandma Jo was escaping down the tree when she wasn't looking. Mom didn't stop to think that Grandma Jo would just parachute down if she had to.

"You can't come to my school, Erma," I said.

"Can so."

"Can not."

"Can so! Who died and made you king of Pennybaker School anyway?"

"I did!"

She hopped off my bed and waltzed to my door, stopping only to turn around and say, "Well, if you're dead, then you won't mind me being there." She stuck out her tongue and was gone.

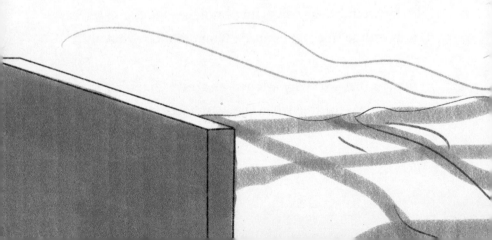

I wasn't sleeping well to begin with—too many nightmares involving Erma at my school—which was probably why the noise woke me up. It was a kind of grating, scraping, bumping noise.

Also, it was cold. I had pulled the blankets up to my nose again. The very tip of my nose felt frozen solid.

I opened my eyes and peered through the darkness.

The window was open.

"What in the world?" I whispered, sitting up. I glanced around. All the shadows in my room looked like they had heads and eyes and mutant claws at the ends of their mutant arms. Everything seemed to be moving. It was funny how a guy's totally normal bedroom turned into a monster convention in the middle of the night.

Slowly, I crept out of bed and tiptoed to the window. I stuck my head through and looked down at the ground.

Nothing.

Nobody in my room, nobody outside my room. Just an open window and a whole lot of cold.

Mom had cut the branches away from outside Grandma Jo's window, but she hadn't done anything to the trellis outside mine.

I slipped my feet into my slippers and padded across the hall. I didn't want to be the one to break it to Mom that she was right about Grandma Jo. But at the same time, I was glad, because if Mom was right, it meant I was right, too. And Grandma Jo was a pretty good liar.

I pushed open Grandma Jo's door, expecting an empty bed and perhaps a few discarded skateboarding kneepads in her place.

Instead, I saw a lump. A Grandma-Jo-shaped lump, curled on her side, her covers pulled up. Her silver hair shivered in the crosswind that came from my room.

I turned back. If it wasn't Grandma Jo opening my window . . .

I returned to my room and shut the window. Then I rummaged around in my closet until I found an old baseball bat from my days playing in the rec league, back before I discovered that nobody likes you when you make their baseball disappear in the bottom of the ninth inning.

I climbed into bed, but instead of lying down, I sat with my back against the headboard and tried not to shake too much.

There was no way I could sleep now. In just hours, Erma would be invading my space. And Mr. Smith would still be at Pennybaker. And Mr. Faboo would still be gone. And there was nothing I could do about any of it.

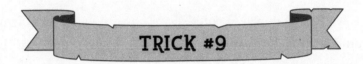

TRICK #9

THE MUTINY MANIFESTATION

"How good do you think you'd be at finding a missing person?" I asked as soon as Chip and I slid out of his mom's car the next morning.

He thought it over. "Superior. Especially if I were to wear a pair of forensics investigation socks."

"Does that mean you'll help me find someone?"

"Sure! Who are we finding?"

"Mr. Faboo," I said. "We need to figure out why he left, and get him back." We pushed into the vestibule, where Clover Prentice was waiting next to the head of horror with her arms crossed—and double crossed—and a big frown on her face.

"Excuse me?" she demanded. She looked pointedly from us to the head and back again.

"I thought you were doing it now," I said to Chip, confused.

"You said it was your job. I specifically remember the words. You said, and I quote—"

"Well, why didn't you tell me that?"

Chip looked genuinely perplexed. "Why would I tell you something that you told me?"

I gestured to the head, which seemed to be extra scowly this morning, like even *it* was mad at me for not polishing it. "Because now nobody got it done."

"Because it's your j—"

"I don't care whose job it is," Clover Prentice shouted. "Just get it done!" She tossed a rag at me, and I caught it. Chip and I looked at each other as she walked away.

Chip brightened. "So I'll start finding some leads."

"Really? Just like that?"

"Like what?"

I shook my head. "Just . . . Never mind. We'll talk about it later." I let my backpack drop to the floor, dipped the rag into the bowl of Chip's (really smelly at this point) homemade polishing agent, and started rubbing it on Helen Heirmauser's hair.

Chip came over and put his hand on top of mine. "I've found that a gentle, circular motion works best. Follow the flow of her curls. Like this." He started to move my hand with his, but I glared at him. "Right. I'll go work on those leads. See you in class."

7

"I hope Mr. Faboo is back," Wesley said. We were walking as a group to Facts After the Fact class, as we always did. "Mr. Smith makes me sleepy." He let his head bob, pretending to fall asleep, complete with loud snores.

"Me, too," Flea said. "I hate to admit it, but I kind of miss the costumes. And the skits."

"And Ye Olde English," Wesley said in an English accent.

"Yeah, that, too," Flea said.

"Well, Mr. Faboo can't be gone forever," Wesley said.

"Technically—"

"Not now, Chip," I said.

We walked through the classroom door and, one by one, our shoulders slumped. Sitting behind Mr. Faboo's desk was Mr. Smith. Only he'd reorganized it, replacing Mr. Faboo's quill and inkwell with regular pencils, and replacing Mr. Faboo's scroll with a boring old desk calendar.

"Come in, please," Mr. Smith said. Even he sounded bored. "The bell is about to ring, and we have lots to discuss."

We filed in and took our seats just as the bell rang. Mr. Smith stood, smoothed out his suit jacket, and went to the blackboard. "Essay Topics," he wrote in really big letters across the top of the board.

"What's an essay?" Colton asked.

Mr. Smith turned and stared at him. "It's a paper. You know, the kind you write in English class."

"English class?" I heard someone whisper, and then someone else responded, "It's what they used to call Lexiconical Arts in the olden days."

"We've never written an essay," Patrice Pillow said. "Mrs. Codex has us write poems or limericks or screenplays or novels. You know, the usual stuff."

"That is not the usual— Never mind," Mr. Smith said. "An essay is a paper discussing a particular topic. In this case, your essay is going to be an informative piece about the character you've chosen for History Month."

"What's History Month?" Buckley asked.

"It's Act After the Fact Month," I said.

"Oh, so you're having us write an essay and then act it out? Brilliant!" Wesley exclaimed. "I haven't really had the chance to do a nonfiction reading."

"No, no, you're going to write a biographical piece about your character," Mr. Smith said. "Like what's in your textbooks."

We all turned and looked at the bookshelf that held our textbooks. The shelf was thick with dust, and the white spines on the books were yellowing. There was a spiderweb stretching across half of them.

"We've never read them," Flea said.

"Yeah, Mr. Faboo says they're way more boring than history. Those books won't tell you that Napoleon once got attacked by rabbits. Or that there was a baboon named Jackie who was promoted to corporal in World War I."

"Or about the ghost ship," Patrice Pillow said.

"The SS *Ourang Medan*," Owen added. "The ship that sent out a desperate SOS, and then when everyone got there . . ."

Wesley made a noise and flopped his head to one side, his tongue hanging out. Very realistic. His acting classes were really paying off.

Samara Lee squeaked and slapped her hands over her eyes.

"No, no, no," Mr. Smith said. "We're not studying ghost ships or rabbits or army baboons. We're studying real history. No . . . nonsense."

We all gasped. Mr. Faboo would have never called those things nonsense.

"But that is real history," Flea said.

"It's not the kind of history we learn in this class," Mr. Smith argued, and again we all gasped.

"Technically," Chip said, "history—and one would assume this denotes what you call 'real history'—is defined as the study of events, particularly in human affairs."

"Exactly!" I said. "And what could be more human than ghosts, rabbits, and baboons?"

"Actual humans?" Wesley said.

"You know what I mean," I muttered.

"I'll tell you what," Mr. Smith said, rocking back on his heels. He scratched one eyebrow. "Since you seem to enjoy definitions so much, Mr. Mason, I'm going to assign you an extra little project for History Month. Let's say you write a paper, five pages, detailing the American Revolution, starting with the first shot at Lexington and going all the way through until you reach Cornwallis at Yorktown." He bent over at the waist so he was looking Chip in the eye. "And don't forget to include lots of definitions."

"But that's not fair," I said.

"Okay, Mr. Fallgrout," Mr. Smith said. "Since you seem so interested in fairness, I'll be expecting the same paper from you."

"What? You can't—"

"Due next Friday."

"But—"

"Now, everyone go grab a textbook and turn to page fifty-three. We'll begin there, and then we'll discuss these essays."

We shuffled toward the dusty, spiderwebby shelf, all looking at one another as if something horrible had just happened. And, in a way, it had.

"When Mr. Faboo finds out about this, he isn't going to like it one bit," Wesley whispered as we bent to pick up our books.

But then Flea whispered what we were all thinking but

were afraid to say. "Let's just face it—Mr. Faboo really isn't coming back."

Thirty minutes later, the bell rang, and we all bolted, many of us leaving our textbooks on our desks, the pages fluttering in our wakes. I had no idea what page I was even on. I'd spent most of my class time thinking—about the essays, about the extra assignment that Chip and I now had to do.

About revolutions.

That was it. We were thinking too small. Finding Mr. Faboo was a big job, and if we intended to get it done, we needed to all-out revolt.

"Can you believe he did that to us?" I railed, catching up with Chip in the hallway. "So not fair."

"Agreed. Mr. Faboo would have never assigned such a paper," Chip said. "He would have known that you can't sum up eight years of bloody battle in just five pages. Eight years of fighting against oppression, of yearning for freedom. Of refusing to bow to the crown. The American spirit! The foundation of our democracy! The very insurrection that this country was built upon! In five pages? I'll need at least twenty."

"Chip. Focus," I said, grabbing his arm and turning him to face me. "We're not writing those papers."

"We've been assigned," he said, confused. "He didn't mention it being optional."

"We're not doing it, because we're going to have our own revolution."

"We are?"

I nodded, putting my arm around him and walking toward the door. "We're going to fight against our own oppressor. We're going to fight against Mr. Smith."

"But how? I'm afraid I don't even own a pair of revolution socks."

I stopped and turned him to face me again. "We're going to find Mr. Faboo and get him back."

2

"Hey, Thomas! Thomas!" Chip was hurrying to catch up with me after the next class. "Look what I found." He held out a postcard. "A clue!"

I took it from him and studied it. "Boone County History-Lovers Society? Where did you find it?"

"In Mr. Faboo's desk drawer," he said proudly. "I clandestinely snuck in and snatched it when Mr. Smith went to the restroom." He beamed.

"You stole it?"

"I found it." His face clouded over. "You're right. I should return it." He took it from my hand, his shoulders sagging guiltily. "I was just so excited to be sleuthing with you again."

"It's okay, Chip," I said, taking the postcard back. "So what are we supposed to do with it?"

His toothy smile returned. "I figured we could look up the events calendar for the Boone County History-Lovers Society and go to a meeting. Surely Mr. Faboo will be there. And then we can get to the bottom of this whole debacle."

I wasn't sure what a debacle was. But I was sure of two things—Chip was kind of a genius, and his plan was perfect.

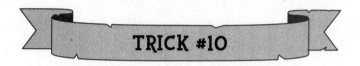

TRICK #10

THE WEB OF TEXTBOOK

"Good news," Chip said the next day, sidling up to me as we walked to Four Square class. "As of last evening, I am a card-carrying member of the Boone County History-Lovers Society. I have my sights set on a leadership role. I have some cutting-edge ideas about properly honoring the founding of Boone County. And, even better news, there is an upcoming event."

"What kind of event?" I asked.

"A Civil War reenactment," Chip said. I stopped.

"A what?"

Chip nodded ferociously. "With rifled muskets and swords and cannons and horses. If Mr. Faboo is the historian I believe him to be, he will be at that reenactment."

"Really?"

"Yep; there's a battle today, and my mom says she'll take us."

I knew I should have been a little skeptical of Chip's ideas, because the only place they ever seemed to really get us was into trouble. And embarrassment. I had learned that much when the Heirmauser head went missing.

But the problem was that Chip's ideas always sounded really awesome. I mean, what guy doesn't want to run around a field with a sword, yelling and fighting without actually getting hurt?

"Okay," I said, despite my own reservations. "Let's reenact the Civil War."

I'd spent an entire week faking nosebleeds and stomachaches and sore knees. But Coach Abel was getting doubtful about my ailments, so it was time to get creative. I came out of the locker room with my pockets weighed down by ten smoke cartridges, but if I kept my T-shirt untucked and pulled down low, they were mostly hidden.

Of course, we weren't supposed to have our T-shirts untucked and pulled down low, so it was the first thing Coach Abel noticed when he saw me.

"Mr. Fallgrout, would you mind dressing according to the rules?" he asked when I joined my squad for calisthenics.

I pretended to be confused. "But I'm wearing the standard-issue shorts and shirt, Coach."

"Yes," he said. "But you're not wearing them correctly."

"I'm kind of hot," I said. "I was thinking since we weren't playing a contact sport—"

"Tuck!" he barked, so I tucked.

I had barely sat down in my squad line when Chip Mason leaned back. "What's in your pockets?" he asked.

My hands immediately flew to my sides. "Nothing."

"Granted, I'm not wearing my telepathic socks, because they're not part of the approved physical-education dress code—which, as you've just been made aware, is extremely important to our coach—but I can clearly see that there's something in your pockets. Not in my mind, of course, like a regular telepath would see it, but with my actual eyes. Nearsightedness notwithstanding." He pushed up his glasses.

"I thought I told you to stop using the word 'notwithstanding,'" I said.

Coach trilled on his whistle and told us to get started on sit-ups. We all fell back. I kept my arms at my sides, pressed against my pockets so the smoke cartridges wouldn't fall out.

"That's not how you do it," Wesley whispered. Like Wesley would know. He was always too busy singing a song from some musical about prisoners to actually do any of the calisthenics.

"My neck hurts," I whispered back. "I need to rest it."

Chip sat up. "Technically, if it's your neck that's aggrieving you, you should lace your hands behind your head to give it support." He modeled a perfect sit-up for me—one time down, one time up. "Did I say 'aggrieving'? I would suppose 'aggravating' would be a better word. Although 'aggravating' assumes a state of mind, and your neck doesn't possess a mind. Though it does have the very esteemed duty of holding one up. Which is quite ironic, when you think about it." He laughed.

"I don't think about it," I said. "Nobody but you thinks about it."

He went back to his sit-ups.

"Hey, what's in your pockets?" Wesley asked, his voice just a little too loud. I shushed him, catching the coach's attention. He looked up, and we all double-timed our sit-ups until he yelled out, "Push-ups, gentlemen," and looked down again.

"If you must know," I whispered, flipping over, "it's a magic trick."

"Cool," Wesley said. "Can I see it?"

"You will, okay? Be patient."

We finished our calisthenics, ran warm-up laps, and waited for the girls to arrive. The chatter got loud as everyone paired off with their dance partners and found a spot on the gym floor with room to move. I stayed rooted to my spot, hoping that maybe Sissy Cork was absent. Or had quit school altogether. Maybe moved out of state. Or to the moon. And took her ballroom dance with her.

No such luck. "You ready?" She had come up behind me. I jumped and whirled around. Her arms were crossed, and she looked about as excited about dancing as I did. "You ready to dance or what?"

"What," I answered, but she had already taken my hand and begun pulling me to a vacant spot on the floor. I pressed my arms to my sides, hoping the cartridges wouldn't rattle when I walked. Once again, my stomach heaved.

"What's your deal?" she asked. "Why are you walking all stiff like that?"

"No reason," I said. "I think I pulled something in my back."

"Oh. I've done that before at a strong-man competition. You know what they say about sore muscles—the best way to make them feel better is to move them."

"She's right," Chip said, as he and Patrice whirled by. Chip was dancing like someone who'd been doing it his whole life, and the music hadn't even started yet. "It's the lactic acid released during strenuous activity. Interesting thing about lactic acid . . ." He kept talking, but Patrice had danced him out of earshot.

"Okay, friends!" the girls' dance coach hollered, clapping her hands together three times. "Let's get started." She reached over and pushed a button. The music started, and everyone began moving, all eyes on Chip to lead them.

The timing was perfect.

"You ready?" Sissy asked, holding out her arms.

All I had to do was . . .

"Hello, Earth to Thomas."

Slip my hand into my pocket . . .

"I'm not going to stand around waiting all day."

Grab a cartridge, squeeze the two sides together, and . . .

There was a long, loud farting noise that made my shorts shiver. Everyone stopped and looked over. The noise was followed by a thin contrail of smoke rising from my backside.

Darn it. That was what I got for using smoke cartridges that had been in a trunk for ten years.

Sissy Cork started to cough, waving her hand in front of her face. "Gross! Did you just—?"

"You guys!" Buckley shouted. "Thomas just ripped one!" He pointed at the smoke. "And it's smoking!"

"No," I said, reaching into my pocket. "It wasn't me."

Sissy coughed again and turned away. "I can't believe you, Thomas Fallgrout."

"It was a smoke cartridge!" I said, pulling out one of the

cartridges. The movement set off another cartridge, and a louder, longer fart noise erupted.

The entire class burst into laughter. Except for Sissy Cork, who crossed her arms and stormed off to the girls' locker room.

Well, at least the trick was successful.

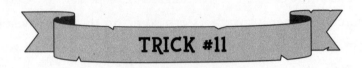

TRICK #11

CAMP CONFUSION

On the way to the reenactment camp, Chip's mom told us all kinds of stories about the Civil War. She told us about a brave slave named Robert Smalls, who stole a Confederate steamship called the CSS *Planter* and delivered it to the Union Navy. She told us about Belle Boyd, who was an amazing Confederate spy. And she told us that 620,000 men died in the Civil War, but a lot of them died from mumps, measles, and malaria rather than gunfire.

Chip was a lot like his mom.

In fact, Chip's mom was planning to join us in the reenactment. She knew a guy who used to be friends with Chip's grandpa Old Huck Mason, and he told her she could be the camp cook. I didn't know why anyone would want to cook with all that awesome battling going on all around, but she seemed really happy to get such a fun job.

The camp was bustling with guys in uniforms, guys in ratty clothes, guys with horses, guys with soot on their faces, guys chewing straw, guys drinking out of Aquafina bottles when nobody was looking, guys doing pretty much everything you could think of. The camp was also filled with women who were cooking things over open fires and shaking out dusty blankets and sewing buttons onto jackets. The air was crisp with burning, crackling wood, and rang with the whinnying of anxious horses tied to trees.

Chip's mom's friend greeted us outside his tent. He was old and craggy and looked a lot like Huck Mason, except not quite as sick. Chip's mom called him Bud.

"Welcome, welcome, y'all," he crowed, climbing out of the tent, his hands extended to each of us. He gave Chip's mom a quick hug and called her Gert—which was weird, because I thought her name was Sherry—and then clapped Chip and me on the back and asked if we were ready to go to war. "Come on over here, now," he said, leading us toward another tent. "We can't have y'all heading out there in Nikes and Levis, now, can we?"

"Technically," Chip said, "Levis weren't invented until 1873, which makes us just a few years too early for them."

"Exactly," Bud said. "Plus, y'all soldiers need uniforms if you're going into battle."

Bud parted the tent flaps, and we ducked inside. It was more of a teepee than a tent, with furry skins laid out all over

95

the floor and trunks overflowing with supplies lining the walls. Bud knelt with a grunt and began pulling clothes out of one of the trunks and tossing them to us. "Pants, shirt, braces."

"Braces?" I asked.

"Suspenders," Chip whispered. "The kind that button into your pants instead of clipping on."

"Here's a whole load of socks," Bud continued, tossing a handful of socks at our feet. "And you'll need these shirts here. And jackets for you Union folks. Those are hanging up over there."

We gazed at a far wall, where three dark-blue military coats hung. They were enormous and would have hung down to our ankles.

"Technically," Chip said, "most of the Confederate Army wore regular clothes rather than uniforms. That was one of the things that made them difficult to spot."

"You are correct, sir," Bud said. He clapped Chip's shoulder twice, and Chip looked really pleased with himself. "Y'all are fightin' for the South, then. Get dressed and meet me outside for instructions. Battle should begin soon, so don't dillydally."

Bud left the tent, and we scrambled around trying to find the right clothes. Nothing fit. Everything was either way too small or way too big. My gut hung out the bottom of my shirt, and my pants didn't want to stay up. What was worse, the braces Bud had handed us were all broken. I was forced to hold on to the waistband of my pants as I walked.

"How am I supposed to go to battle like this?" I asked. "I can't do everything one-handed."

We filed out of the tent, blinking in the sun.

"Keep your eyes peeled for Mr. Faboo," I said. I tried to peer under the brim of every hat for a familiar face, but it occurred to me that without his typical white wig and tights, I might not recognize him. He'd never come to class dressed as a Civil War soldier.

The rest of the camp had already cleared out, and I could see Bud standing with a group of guys off in the distance. He waved me over while a lanky man pulled the bluecoats aside. I jogged to Bud.

"Okay, now. In a minute, someone will blow a horn. When you hear that horn, you just follow me, and I'll keep you safe. The last thing you want is to be separated from your unit, you hear?" I nodded. "If someone tells you that you've been hit, you need to fall down and keep real still and wait for the battle to be over. But do not get hit. Got it?"

"Got it."

I stood there, energy buzzing through me as I contemplated what my plan of action would be. I would storm the front line, sweep around the back, and—

The horn blasted, and everyone sprang into action, running every which way, shouting orders. Bud had assured us that the guns fired only blanks—no real bullets—but I didn't expect blanks to be so loud. I jumped every time one went off, and I wasn't even close to any of them.

Basically, I was the worst soldier ever. I stood in one place, whipping my head from side to side, trying to figure out what to do or where to go. "Mr. Faboo?" I cried, but my voice was lost in the noise. "Mr. Faboo?"

"Run!" I heard, and turned just in time to see Chip barreling toward me, holding his hat on his head with both hands, a terrified expression on his face. "Run, man! Forget Faboo! Save yourself!"

I sprinted past him, though I had no real idea where I was going. I thought I could see Bud ahead of me, but the men

had all started to kind of look alike, and when the man turned, he wasn't Bud at all. I veered left, only to find myself heading right toward another stranger in a blue jacket. I wheeled back the way I'd come and discovered that Chip was gone. I spun in place, breathing heavily, twitching, gripping the waistband of my pants. Everywhere was chaos, and even though I knew this was all fake, a part of me was genuinely scared. It must have been really frightening to actually be on a battlefield.

"Run!" I heard again, out of nowhere, and Chip whizzed past me, this time going the other way. "Move, move, move!"

Just as my muscles tensed to make a run for it, there was a huge blast right behind me. I turned to find three men wheeling a cannon in my direction.

I squealed just like Erma does when something gross touches her, and my feet began churning and my arms pumping without me even telling them to.

To be honest, I wasn't sure who exactly won our simulated battle. I only know that I spent the second half of it hiding behind a tree on the edge of the field. A dog found its way to me, and I sat on the ground and scratched its ears while the chaos raged on in the distance. I guessed I wasn't much of a soldier.

Don't get me wrong—Chip wasn't much better. It was just that he didn't give up. He continued to race around the field, yelling and running, yelling and running. After a while, a horn sounded, and everyone stopped in place, red-faced and panting, their uniforms soaked through with sweat. They took off their hats and fanned themselves with them. A couple got out their cell phones and answered texts. Finally, a chance to get a good look at faces.

"Dinnertime!" Mrs. Mason called from over by the food tent, and everyone converged on it at once.

"I can't find him," I whispered to Chip as we stood in the chow line.

"Who?"

"Mr. Faboo. I don't see him anywhere."

"Oh. Yeah. Mr. Faboo. I forgot."

"What y'all whisperin' about over there?" Bud asked, leaning toward us as he walked to a picnic table with an aluminum plate heaped with beans and hot dogs.

"Do you know where Mr. Faboo is?" I asked.

"Mr. Fa-who?" Bud squinted like he was thinking really hard.

"Faboo. He's . . ." I started to describe him, but realized it was impossible to describe someone if you've never really paid attention to what they looked like. "He wears a white wig sometimes?"

"A white wig? No, I can't say I've ever seen anyone like that, except maybe Old Tony over there." He gestured toward a really old man with a mop of sweaty, snow-white hair flopping over one eye.

"No, it's not like that. It's more . . ." I used my hands to indicate the poofiness of Mr. Faboo's favorite wig.

"He's our teacher," Chip said. "At Pennybaker School."

"Oh, that feller," Bud said. "Sorry, boys, he is no more."

Chip gasped. "He's dead?"

"Dead? Oh, heavens no. Who said anything about dead?

He just doesn't do Civil War reenactment anymore. Something about the braces giving him a rash or some such. He was a good Union fighter, too. Knew everything there was to know about history."

"Do you have any idea where we might find him?" I asked.

"Nope, can't say I do. Sorry, fellers."

"Oh," I said, but inside I was totally dashed. We'd come all this way and fought two hard battles for nothing.

Mr. Faboo was still missing.

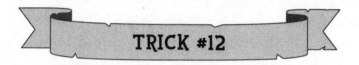

TRICK #12

DEALING DETENTION

Chip was teaching another early-morning dance class, so I had Dad drive me to school extra early so I could polish the Heirmauser head and have it already shiny when Clover Prentice and her crossy-crossy arms got there.

I had just come out of the custodian's closet with my supplies when Chip, Wesley, Flea, and Owen entered the school. Chip said something, and they all laughed. They got to the bottom of the stairs, quickly bowed to the Heirmauser head, and then got up and huddled in a loose circle. One by one, they began an elaborate handshake, twisting their fingers, bumping their knuckles, flashing peace signs, and slapping and gripping and knocking their shoulders together. It took about five solid minutes to complete. I stopped and watched, dumbfounded.

A few weeks earlier, Chip had asked if I wanted to create

a special handshake with him. He'd proposed it at the lunch table, and all the guys had snickered so hard that someone— although nobody would confess to being the culprit—hacked a half-chewed cucumber onto the table.

"Uh, right, that's what babies do," I had said, rolling my eyes really hard, even though I'd immediately thought of some handshake ideas that would look pretty great.

"Oh," Chip had said. He'd pushed up his glasses and let it go.

Had I known the other guys were going to decide that fancy handshakes were actually really cool, I might have changed my mind about the babyishness of it. Of course, that was something my mom would have called "being a fol- lower," and "being a follower" almost always tended to "get a boy in trouble." And then she would start talking about stuff they used to say in the old days when there must have been a lot more people jumping off bridges for fun than there are now.

I cleared my throat loudly. Chip glanced at me, then finished his ritual before peeling away from the group.

"Why are you here so early, Thomas?" he asked.

"I have a job to do," I said haugh- tily. I walked to

the statue and took the cap off the polish. The real polish, not Chip's nasty homemade licking polish.

"Oh, I've got it," he said, reaching for the rag.

I snatched it back from him. "No. It's my job."

"But I can do it," he said, yanking on the other end of the rag. I refused to let go. The rag was pulled taut between us like a tug-of-war rope.

"No. You. Can't." I jerked right back. He stumbled into the pedestal, making the head wobble in its spot. We both watched with fear, but it settled back into place.

"I do it every day," he said, yanking again. "When I didn't do it, it didn't get done."

"But you're not supposed to," I said, pulling back—only this time I pulled with all my might, causing Chip to knock hard into the pedestal. Instead of just wobbling now, the statue wheeled, tipping, tipping. We both let go of the rag, letting it fall to the floor, and reached for the head.

But we were too late.

I watched as the bust left the pedestal and tumbled in slow motion down and down and down. It landed on the tile floor with a heavy crunching sound, and then rolled right onto a pair of feet. Mr. Smith's feet, to be exact. It came to a stop on its back. There was a huge dent in its forehead, and the nose was gone.

Mr. Smith studied the head as if he couldn't figure out how it had gotten there, and then turned his angry, red face toward us.

"Gentlemen." He pointed sternly toward the office. "Come with me. Looks like we have a detention to schedule."

7

I didn't speak to Chip all day. And Chip didn't speak to me. When you started in Principal Rooster's office getting detention, you knew you were going to be in for a long day, and it was a really, really long day. We were even silent on the ride home. All I could think about was how I was in trouble at school and would be in trouble at home, and how it was all Chip's fault. If he had just stopped trying to steal my job— and my friends—none of this would have happened. Why did he have to be so perfect at everything? It made regular guys like me look *really* not perfect. And regular guys like me didn't need any help in that department. Most of the time I was doing a perfect job of reminding the world how not perfect I was.

I could hear arguing coming from the kitchen as soon as I walked through the front door. I dropped my backpack at the bottom of the stairs and loosened my bow tie.

Erma was sitting on the bottom step, eating a bowl of ice cream.

"What's going on?" I asked. "Why are you eating here?"

She didn't look up; she just kept shoveling the ice cream into her mouth. "Mom sent me out of the kitchen," she said, "on account of Grandma Jo's tattoo."

"What tattoo? Grandma Jo has a tattoo?"

Erma shrugged. "That's pretty much what Mom said, too." I pulled off my vest, dropped it on top of my backpack, and started toward the kitchen. "I wouldn't go in there if I were you."

I snuck through the living room and peered into the kitchen. Mom was standing in front of Grandma Jo with her arms crossed, tapping her foot. She had that look that she always got when she was getting ready to go on a You Will Not Lie to Me, Young Man Adventure.

Trust me—that was not a good adventure to go on.

"You've had it all this time, and I just didn't notice it, huh?" Mom was saying. "You've been my mother for my whole life, and I haven't seen that tattoo."

"I guess not," Grandma Jo said. The sleeve of her sweater was pushed up to reveal a brightly colored picture of what looked like a llama riding a motorcycle. That was definitely noticeable.

"When did you get it? You haven't left the house in days."

"Exactly! That's what I've been trying to tell you. How could I get a new tattoo when I'm here all the time?"

Mom tapped her foot harder, and her eyebrows got closer together. Grandma Jo let her sleeve drop over the llama. I'd never seen Grandma Jo look nervous before. When you made Grandma Jo look nervous, you were being really scary.

Mom shook her finger at Grandma Jo. "I'm watching you," she said. "I will figure out what you're doing. Mark my words!"

Grandma Jo picked up a glass of iced tea and handed it to Mom. "You look awfully flushed, dear. Are you hot?"

Mom grabbed the iced tea, huffed, and took a drink.

This was definitely not the right time to tell her about the detention I'd just gotten.

Normally, I was pretty much on Grandma Jo's side when Mom was trying to baby her. I hated to be babied, too. But now I was certain Grandma Jo was the one opening my window at night.

She thought she could fool me. But she wasn't the only one who could be sneaky.

I wasn't sure I could solve the mystery of the missing Mr. Faboo. But I was pretty sure I could solve this one, if I just kept trying.

Grandpa Rudy had a black cloth that he called his floating cloth. He used it whenever he wanted to hide something from the audience. Sometimes that would be something small, like a ball or Bill the rabbit. Sometimes it would be something big, like his assistant, Irene. Irene was great at getting lost. So great that one time Grandpa Rudy made her disappear in a show and she never came back, just like Bill the rabbit. But Grandma Jo said that had a lot more to do with Irene's "poor work ethic" than Grandpa Rudy's magic skills. I wasn't sure exactly what that meant. But once when I was at the grocery store with Grandma Jo we ran into Irene, so I knew she wasn't floating out in a parallel universe or something.

Grandpa Rudy's cloth smelled like his aftershave. Probably because he used to like to wipe the sweat off the back of his neck with it. Every so often, when I was feeling lonely, I would get out Grandpa Rudy's floating cloth and smell it, remembering sitting on Grandpa Rudy's lap while he practiced card tricks.

Tonight, though, my trick wasn't so much magical as it was sneaky. After dinner—a very cold, uncomfortable dinner, where Mom stared at Grandma Jo's llama and Dad stared at Mom, and I opened my mouth a hundred times to tell them about my detention and never could make it come out—I tiptoed into the garage and pulled an armload of empty cans out of the recycling bin. Quietly, I took them upstairs and lined them up along my window ledge. Then I hung the black cloth over the cans and secured it to the top of the window.

My work done, I turned off the light and stepped back. It looked like a dark night outside, not a cloth hiding a booby trap. It was perfect. I could hardly wait to get to bed so I could catch Grandma Jo in the act.

⌒

I could see my breath when I woke. I sat up, and five cans, which had been lined up along the edge of my blanket, clattered against one another as they fell to the floor.

What I didn't see anywhere was the black cloth.

Or Grandma Jo.

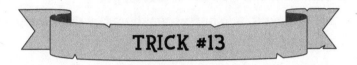

TRICK #13

THE PARTY PINCH

Dad was fidgeting with the thermostat when I got out of the bathroom. I'd made my morning shower hot and steamy to try to thaw out my nose.

"I don't think this thing is working," he said, tapping the numbers on the front. "Does it feel chilly in here to you, pal?"

I shrugged. "I guess."

He pulled off the cover, peered at the mechanical guts, and then blew into them. Dad's method of fixing everything from a smashed finger to a broken dishwasher started with blowing on it. Basically, Dad wasn't very good at fixing things at all. His method went like this:

1. **Blow on it and murmur something about dust.**
2. **Scratch head, wondering aloud, "What could**

have possibly happened? It was just working yesterday."

3. Search in the garage for a tool, get sidetracked, and end up washing the driveway instead.
4. Get really red and shiny when Mom yells about the thing never being fixed.
5. Blow on it again.
6. Tap it a few times with a tool—any tool will do.
7. Say, "Must have been the kids," and then pretend to hurt finger/toe/elbow/shoulder/ankle in the repair effort.
8. Call someone professional to come fix it.

Sometimes Mom would mess up his system by pushing him out of the way. Mom's method of fixing things:

1. Say, "I have to do everything myself."
2. Push Dad out of the way.
3. Stare at the broken thing.
4. Call someone professional to come fix it.

Mom's method was a little more streamlined than Dad's.

"Are we sure there's not a window left open somewhere?" Dad yelled, closing one eye and leaning in really close to stare at the thermostat.

"I checked all the windows!" Mom hollered back. Good thing I closed mine before getting in the shower.

"Well, I guess I'd better go find a tool," Dad said, putting the cover back on.

"Dad," I said. "I need to tell you something." I didn't want to come clean about my detention, but I sort of had to.

"Can it wait, pal? You know your mother hates it when I get sidetracked from fixing something."

"No . . . I mean, yes. Sure." I sighed as I watched Dad walk to the garage. I was such a chicken.

I headed to the kitchen. Saturday was the only day of the week that Mom didn't make breakfast—which meant we could eat toaster waffles with loads of syrup and whipped cream and butter and sprinkles and chocolate chips, and she wouldn't do anything about it.

That was exactly what Grandma Jo was eating when I got to the kitchen.

"Good morning," she said around a mouthful of waffle.

"Hey," I said, eyeing her carefully. "Are you cold?" I asked casually.

She pointed at her waffle with her fork. "Warm and toasty," she said. "You should get yourself a nice, hot waffle, too." She patted her belly. "Warms you from the inside out."

I found a waffle in the freezer—the last one in the box—and dropped it into the toaster. "So . . . what did you do last night?"

"Why do you ask?"

"Just curious," I said. I kept my back to her. "Don't know if you watched a good show or played a game of solitaire or, you know, got another new tattoo."

When I turned around, she was grinning at me, a dollop of whipped cream on her chin like a tiny beard. "I'm afraid my tattoo days are a thing of the past," she said. "I'm an old lady, you know."

I squinted at her. "You didn't have that tattoo a week ago."

She squinted back. "But you're not one hundred percent sure, are you?" she said. "Part of you thinks it's possible that I might have gotten it a few months or even a few years ago. After all, I wear a lot of sweaters. As an old, tired, frail lady should."

The thing about Grandma Jo was that she probably had a rock concert T-shirt on under that sweater, but you would never know it, because she was a good actor when she wanted to be. So good, in fact, that part of me started to think maybe she did have the llama motorcycle tattoo all along. She was right—I couldn't be 100 percent certain.

My waffle popped up, making me jump. Grandma Jo chuckled.

"Besides," she said as soon as I turned my back, "your mother would never have let me out of the house for something like that."

"That wouldn't stop you from sneaking out," I said. I smeared peanut butter across my waffle.

This time she laughed hard. "Oh, Thomas, you sure have a heck of an imagination. Me, sneaking out."

"It's true," I said, drowning my waffle with syrup. "That's why it's been so cold in here. Because you've been leaving my window open."

She laughed harder. "I'm climbing in and out of windows now? I can barely get up off the floor." We both knew that wasn't true. We both knew that Grandma Jo could practically jump up off the floor onto her toes if that was what she wanted to do. "You really need to read more books, Tommy. Engage that imagination of yours with something worthwhile, rather than silly theories. And besides—"

She was interrupted by the doorbell.

"You finish making your waffle," she said, holding out a hand to stop me from moving toward the door. "I'm done. I'll get it." She scooted her chair back, dabbed at the corners of her mouth with her napkin, stuffed it into her sweater pocket, and then was off.

She was out of the room before I realized that the napkin she'd used was black. And looked an awful lot like Grandpa Rudy's floating cloth.

When Grandma Jo came back, she was followed by Chip, even though I'd told her a billion times never to let him come inside without asking me first. He was a good friend and all, but letting him inside was like letting in a cloud of flies—into everything and impossible to get rid of.

"Thomas!" Chip cried. "Salutations on this fine Saturday. The air is crisp! The sun is fulgent! The day is unfurling into something quite dandy! Don't you agree?"

My eye twitched. "What is the sun full of?"

"Fulgent! Bright! Brilliant! Daaazzling!" He danced in a circle, accidentally bumping into the edge of my plate and sending my waffle flying through the air. It splatted on his shoe. "Drat. Right on my carousing socks."

"That was our last waffle, Chip."

"Oh," he said. He pushed his glasses up on his nose, looking very serious as he shook the waffle off his foot. He brightened. "Not to worry. You're welcome to partake of my mom's homemade organic, gluten-free, vegan sweet-potato muffins. Come on, I'll take you." He reached out to grab my arm, but I leaned away.

"Gross, no. And I've told you a thousand times to stop saying 'partake.' You sound like an old-timey novel. And a sweet-potato muffin is not a substitute for a waffle." My stomach growled, as if even it was angry with Chip. "Besides," I said, bending to pick my breakfast up off the floor, "I'm still mad at you."

"For what? Oh, for that little mishap with the broken bust? Don't worry, Thomas, detention isn't—"

"Shhh!" I said, slapping my hand over his mouth, but it was too late. Mom, whose supersonic hearing could pick up words like "broken" and "detention" from a thousand miles away, yelled, "What detention?" from the living room.

I sighed, listening as her footsteps got closer to the kitchen. "What detention?" she repeated. Dad trailed in behind her.

"Hello, Mrs. Fallgrout," Chip said. "Salutations on this—"

"Not now, Chip," Mom and I said at the same time. His mouth clapped shut.

"What detention? I'm not going to ask again."

I had a feeling I was about to be going on a Your Weekend Is So Not Going to Be Fun Adventure. I started to answer, but Chip beat me to it.

"There was a slight accident during a scuffle in the foyer at our esteemed alma mater."

"Scuffle?" Mom said, looking alarmed. "At school? Accident?"

Great. When Mom starts asking questions in rapid fire, there really is no good answer to any of them. "It wasn't a big deal," I said.

"Quite the contrary," Chip said. "I didn't take it personally when Thomas attacked me. Jealousy can cause one to act in an unpredictable manner."

"Attacked?" Mom yelped at the same time I said, "I didn't attack you."

"It's okay," Chip said. "I've forgiven your indiscretion."

"I did not indiscresh anyone, Mom," I said. "I swear."

Chip's finger flew up in the air. "Technically, 'indiscresh' isn't a word. You were probably looking for 'discredit,' although that would not exactly be proper in this sentence, either, and—"

"Shut up, Chip!" I yelled.

"Thomas!" Mom barked. "You can't talk to a guest that way. Apologize to Chip right this instant."

"No way," I said. "I didn't attack him. He stole my job. He *attacked* my job."

"I'm wondering if you might mean 'hijacked' in this particular situation," Chip said.

"No matter what he did with your job, there's no good reason to attack someone," Dad said. "You can't go around attacking people, Thomas."

"I didn't!"

"The only casualty was the Heirmauser statue, anyway," Chip said. He winked at me like he was helping me out. Clearly, he didn't know Mom.

Her eyes grew big as her lips tightened. "The statue? Again?"

"The nose will reattach easily," Chip said.

I didn't think it was possible, but Mom's eyes grew even wider. "You broke her nose off? Oh, Thomas, what is it with you and that statue?"

"He thinks it's a head of horror," Chip said. He made a wide-mouthed, bulgy-eyed face that actually pretty accurately mimicked the statue.

"You're not helping," I said through gritted teeth.

"You should probably go, Chip," Dad said. "Sounds like Thomas has some explaining to do."

I glared at Chip.

"Oh. Okay. But if I may be so bold, I came over to propose a social opportunity for Thomas."

"A what?" Dad said.

"I'm hosting a shindig tonight. We will have snacks and listen to music and possibly play games. My charades socks are freshly laundered and ready to go."

"Are you saying you're having a party?" Mom asked.

"No," I said.

"Actually, yes," Chip said. "Thomas, your mother is a much better listener than you are."

"I mean no, I don't want to go to your party. I don't even want to see you again until Monday. I need a Chip break."

"Thomas," Mom said. "Now you're just being rude. First you attack the boy, and then you insult him? I raised you better than this."

"No," I repeated, ignoring Mom. I put my hand on Chip's back and moved him toward the front door. "No. No. Definitely not."

I opened the door and pushed until Chip was outside. "But don't you want to hear about—"

"No." Okay, actually, I kind of did want to go to his party. But sometimes when you're mad you start talking, and next thing you know, it's too late to turn things around without having to admit all kinds of embarrassing things about being wrong and sorry and stuff. "I don't want to go to your party."

I shut the door in his face.

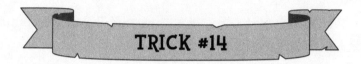

I SHALL NOW PUT ON THESE SHACKLES

Everyone was at Chip's party.

Everyone.

Flea, Owen, Wesley, Patrice Pillow, Samara Lee, Buckley, Dawson Ethan—even Sissy Cork was there.

I knew this because they spent about half an hour knocking on my window and running away every time I went to open it. And there was the *boom boom* beat of music coming from a stereo propped in Chip's window, and I saw them all dance and play football and eat pizza in his front yard and garage. Chip's mom had gotten out a fire pit so everyone could keep warm, and I watched as they all ate gooey s'mores. At one point, even Erma was there. *Erma.* As if it wasn't bad enough that Chip was stealing all my friends, my sister had to be in on it, too?

After the s'mores, Wesley came to my window.

"What?" I said through the glass.

He made an open-up motion with his arms. I shook my head.

"Why don't you come over?" he said, his voice coming through muffled and dim.

"Because I don't want to," I said, even though I really did want to. Really, really bad.

"Chezzisay."

"What?"

"Chezzisay."

"I can't hear you."

He cupped his hands around his mouth. "Chezz-is-say."

"I can't . . ." Exasperated, I threw open the window, just as he took in a deep breath and bellowed.

"Chip. Says. It's. Okay."

I slapped my hands over my ears.

"Oh. Sorry," Wesley said. "I was using my theater voice. What do you think?"

What I thought was that he could stand right where he was in my yard and be heard by an audience in Detroit, but I didn't say that out loud. "You projected," I said, because I knew that, to Wesley, projecting was a life goal.

He beamed. "Thanks. You should come over. Chip says it's okay for you to join us. He forgives you."

"He forgives me?" I asked incredulously. "*He.* Forgives

me." Wesley nodded. "He's the one who got me in trouble in the first place. If he would've just left the statue alone . . ."

"You shouldn't be so hard on him, Thomas," Wesley said. "We all think he's a really cool guy." He said the last in a cartoony voice while swinging his arm and snapping his fingers.

"I know what you all think. If you'll remember, I was the one who became his friend first."

"Exactly." He stood primly and cleared his throat. His Mary Poppins stance. "So you would think you'd be a little easier on the poor fellow."

Just then, the music switched over to our ballroom dancing sound track. Everyone partnered up, including Sissy Cork, who was dancing with Chip. The crackers I'd eaten as a snack a few minutes before lurched around in my stomach.

"Tell Chip I'll see him in detention," I said. I shut the window and the shades.

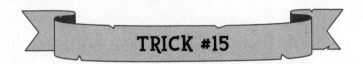

TRICK #15

THE CANNONBALL CRIMP

Erma was at Pennybaker, being fawned over by a group of eighth graders, when I arrived Monday morning. Dad had brought her early to work on the dance, and Mom was going to pick her up and take her to her school when she dropped me off.

"Erma," I said. She ignored me. "Erma." Nothing. "Erma!"

The entire group stared at me with irritated scowls on their faces.

"Jeez, magic boy, chill out," an eighth-grade girl said.

"Yeah. You shouldn't talk to Ermie like that," said another girl with really long, really red fingernails.

"Ermie?"

Erma flipped her hair over one shoulder. "It's my nickname," she said. "You have a problem with that, *magic boy?*" The entire group of girls giggled with her.

I sighed. I didn't have it in me to fight with Erma.

Especially not in front of everyone at Pennybaker, who apparently thought she was the most amazing thing since Chip Mason, and definitely not while Mom was sitting at the curb in her car. The last thing I needed was to have a Being Chewed Out by Your Mom in Front of the Entire School Adventure.

"Whatever. Mom's here."

I walked away, not waiting to see if Erma moved. Let her

deal with Mom. I had to get to class. I trudged up the front stairs and got to the top just as someone came down. In the little sliver of open door, I could see Chip, polishing the pedestal where the head normally sat. Of course.

Instead of going in, I veered off to the right and ducked behind the bushes. Reap was tossing hunks of bread while making strange noises, just like always. I crawled over to him and crouched down.

"Well?"

"Shhh," he said. "I think I'm close to getting her to come out."

"Her?"

"Or him. I won't know until I figure out what dialect we're speaking. It's weird. Not quite badger, and definitely not weasel. It's like weasel with an otter accent. I just can't place it." He made some more clicking noises.

"You really should hang out with Chip," I mumbled, but when he said "Huh?" I didn't repeat myself, because the truth was Reap was the only one of my friends who wasn't hanging out with Chip right now, and I kind of wanted to keep it that way, even if he spent way more time speaking weasel than English.

"Hey, I heard you got detention," Reap said.

"Yeah."

"For throwing Mrs. Heirmauser's head out the window?"

"What? No. Where did you hear that?"

"Just from people. They said you were aiming at Chip Mason. Not true?"

Not that I wouldn't like to sometimes, but . . . "No."

"So why did you get detention?"

"For breaking her nose. And denting her forehead. But it was an accident, I swear."

"So it's not true that you and Chip are enemies now?"

I thought about Chip spilling the beans about my detention, and about avoiding his party. It had been days since we'd ridden our bikes together or pilfered Erma's candy stash, and it had been forever since he'd bugged me to show him a magic trick. Now he was practicing special handshakes with other guys and dancing on the lawn without me and causing me to get detention. "I don't know," I said, and for some reason that made me feel sad.

The warning bell rang, and Reap tossed what was left of the bread under the bush. I saw a black paw reach out and drag a piece farther under. I pointed. "Hey!"

Reap looked. "What?"

"I saw a paw. A black paw."

Reap scratched his chin. "A black paw, you say? Hmm. Maybe it is a badger after all. I'll have to brush up on my Bornean ferret-badger-ese. I'm a bit rusty."

"Yep, you really should hang out with Chip," I repeated.

"Are you going to actually dance today?" Sissy Cork said when our Four Square classes combined.

"Why wouldn't I?" I asked, although I could think of about five thousand reasons why I wouldn't.

1. **I still had a pantyhose rash.**
2. **My toes were too crooked.**
3. **I had an itchy ear.**
4. **I was allergic to music.**
5. **That whole knocking-an-old-lady-into-a-wedding-cake thing.**

"Heads up!" I heard, and looked up just in time to see a basketball whizzing toward my face. I ducked, and it slammed into the folded-up bleachers, getting stuck there.

Sissy Cork was standing with her arms out expectantly, as if a ball hadn't almost just killed me and it would be totally okay for us to just start waltzing around the room. She shook her arms at me impatiently.

"Sorry, I have to get that," I said. I took off before she could argue and scrambled up a stack of floor mats. I wrenched the ball out from between the benches and stood on one, holding the ball high over my head.

"Right here," I heard, and saw an older boy coming toward me with his hands raised.

"I'll bring it down."

"Just throw it," said another boy, who had sidled up to join his friend.

I looked nervously at the stacked mats. They followed my gaze and then elbowed each other. The second boy smiled widely. "Hey, I have an idea," he said.

"Are you thinking what I'm thinking?" the first boy said to his friend.

"Trick shot?"

"Trick shot." The first boy placed his hands on his hips and stared at me defiantly. "Bet you can't do a cannonball onto those mats and shoot a basket at the same time."

My eyes darted from the mat to the basketball goal to Sissy Cork and back to the basketball goal. "Of course I can."

"And make it," the second boy said.

Make it? That was a different matter. But then the music started, and everyone began pairing off to dance. *Hurry up,* Sissy mouthed to me. Which definitely made me want to try whatever trick shot would get me out of dancing the longest.

"And make it," I said. "Totally."

The two older boys laughed and elbowed each other, then stared back at me expectantly. "Go."

I rolled my neck and shoulders and made a big deal of lining up the shot just right, even closing one eye and sticking out my tongue in concentration.

"Go!" the other boy said.

"Hang on, I need to tie my shoe." I bent down, but as soon as my knee hit the bleacher, the first boy spoke up again.

"In five seconds, or it doesn't count."

"No, wait, I—"

"Five . . . four . . . three . . . two . . ."

I closed my eyes and jumped, tucking my knees into my chest and launching the ball blindly into space. I heard an *oof* as the ball landed on someone, but had only milliseconds to open my eyes and realize that person was Coach Abel before I landed on a slab of concrete.

Or at least that was what the mat felt like: concrete, with no cushion whatsoever. The breath was knocked out of me as my rear end lit up with pain. *Ow, ow, ow,* I wanted to say, but nothing came out. The two older boys scrambled away as Coach stomped toward me and I rolled around on the mat holding my rear end.

Another reason I could not dance:

6. I had a bruised butt.

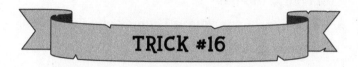

I SHALL NOW HATCH THIS PLAN

Mom wouldn't let me go home, citing that a bruised tailbone due to trying to get out of dancing with a perfectly nice girl was no reason to shirk responsibilities such as school and detention. She told Nurse Hale to give me a pain reliever, and then it was back to class for me. Which meant a whole day of squatting over chairs rather than sitting in them, and listening to about a billion butt jokes.

Some of the Finer Examples of Derriere Humor at Pennybaker School

1. Hey, Thomas, I've heard ballroom dancing is a sport you can really . . . get behind.
2. You know why you couldn't ever be a pirate, Thomas? Because you'd break your booty!

3. I hope you didn't get a crack!
4. You don't have to be so cheeky about ballroom dancing, Thomas.
5. Hey, guys, guess where Thomas sits in his Four Square squad? At the rear!

Chip messed up that last one by pointing out that, technically, I sat third from the rear, and it was Harvey Hinkle who sat at the rear of our squad line. Because Chip didn't usually get normal jokes. He got the kind of jokes that Mom liked to call "clever" and Grandma Jo liked to call "nerdy."

The only thing that could have made my long, horrible day even longer was detention. I trudged into the detention room right after the final bell and slumped into a desk, only to pop right up again, hissing through my teeth at the pain, and then lower myself gently back into the seat.

I could hear the hallway commotion of kids leaving for the day, loudly making plans to do this or that after school. Wesley was heading to rehearsal. Some of the guys were meeting up for football in the park. A couple of girls squealed about how exciiited they were to seeee a certain moviiie starring a certain boooy. Why did girls always use so many vowels when they were looking forward to something? A few kids mentioned getting together with Erma to practice their dancing. Gross.

Soon there was a shuffling at the door, and Chip came in. He eyed me curiously before going to the opposite side of the room and setting his books on a desk as far away from me as he possibly could.

"Wait, *you're* mad at *me*?" I asked. He didn't respond. "You. Are mad. At me?" Still nothing. "Let me tell you, Chip. I'm the one who should be mad at you. You're the reason I'm here."

He turned. "I believe you are the reason I'm here."

"Wow, that actually sounded like a real sentence that a real human would speak."

"Technically, only an English-speaking human," he corrected. "And it's the truth. You've been angry with me ever since we were tasked with the dancing assignment. Which is quite unfair, as I did not create nor implement said assignment. And as I also offered to help you learn to dance many times over."

"Over what?"

"What?"

"Many times over what?"

"Over dancing."

"Huh?"

"What?"

But before we could continue, Mr. Smith came into the room, with his boring brown suit and boring brown shoes and boring brown briefcase.

"No talking, please," he said. "Unless you want to spend more time with me here."

"I wouldn't mind," Chip said. "I'm sure you're an unobjectionable conversationalist."

I didn't know what that meant, but part of me was pretty sure Chip was going to get more detention for name-calling.

"Silence, please," was all Mr. Smith said in response. Maybe he didn't know what it meant, either.

We sat in silence for what seemed like forever, the only sounds the ticking of the clock on the wall and Mr. Crumbs's tile buffer out in the vestibule. I spent the time thinking about what Chip had said about how I was the cause of us being here, that he was the one who was mad at me, and that I'd been pushed to the side by all my friends since we got the dance assignment. I thought about how crazy Chip used to make me, and how it was weird that I was upset about him being upset. And that I didn't like being mad at him, partly because being mad was kind of exhausting, but mostly because without even realizing it, somehow I'd gone from tolerating Chip to actually liking him, and I wasn't sure what to do with myself if I didn't have him to hang around with. And, more than that, I thought about how this whole Chip-and-detention business was distracting me from the real problem at hand: Mr. Faboo's disappearance.

After a while, Mr. Smith pushed back his chair and

sauntered out into the hallway. As soon as he left, I whispered at Chip to get his attention.

"Psst. Psst."

He didn't look back.

"*Pssssssst.*"

He continued to sculpt a paperclip he'd found into a work of art only he could see.

"Psst! Chip! Psst!"

He turned, surprise on his face. "You were talking to me?"

I looked around. "Who else would I be talking to?"

"Oh. Right."

I took a deep breath. "Listen. I'm sorry, okay?"

He thought it over. "Okay."

I scooted my desk a few feet closer and leaned toward him. "Do you have any new leads?"

"About what?"

Seriously? "About Mr. Faboo. The Civil War thing didn't work out, but maybe the Boone County History-Lovers are doing something else. We know for sure now that he's a member, and now you're a member, and they probably have more meetings coming up."

He bit his thumbnail—thinking, thinking—and then poked his finger in the air. "Eureka!"

"Yeah?" I leaned in.

"I'll go to another meeting and find out!"

"That was my idea."

"No, it wasn't. You said we knew he and I were co-members, and you said that the Boone County History-Lovers Society would likely be having another meeting, but you never specifically said that I should attend said meeting. That part was my idea."

"I was insinuating—"

"Oh! Great word! You must be washing your vocabulary socks more often."

Mr. Smith came back into the room, jingling his boring change in his boring pocket. He stopped, examining me. "Mr. Fallgrout, I believe your desk was over there when I left." He pointed at the spot where I'd been before scooting toward Chip.

"Sorry," I murmured, moving back.

"So I suppose this means the two of you had a little chat while I was gone. Despite the fact that I specifically said no talking."

"It wasn't really a chat," Chip said. "It was much shorter than what most would consider a proper chat. Just a few sentences, in fact."

Mr. Smith's lips went into a straight line. "Defiance now, too, Mr. Mason?"

"No. I was simply suggesting that our very short few sentences were not a friendly and informal conversation, such as is the definition of chatting. If you'd stayed out of the room longer, perhaps we could have achieved chat status, but as you returned rather quickly, we—"

"Chip!" I whispered. The timer on Mr. Smith's desk went off.

"May we be excused?" Chip asked.

Mr. Smith grunted, and we hightailed it out of there.

Once in the hallway, I slung my arm around Chip's shoulders. "Chip, I think you had a great idea in there. It's time for another meeting. And it's time we got help."

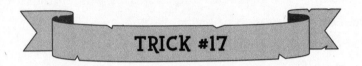

TRICK #17

THE ABANDONMENT ANGLE

Sissy Cork was at my house when I got home. She was standing in the living room with Erma, a familiar, horrible ballroom dancing song playing softly in the background while Erma counted aloud—"One, two, three, four, one, two, three, four, one . . ."

Erma was wearing one of her dance costumes—a pink thing with a big, foofy skirt. Worse than that, Sissy was wearing one of Erma's dance costumes, too—a white thing with a bigger, foofier skirt. She scowled at me when I walked in the door.

"It's about time," she said. "I've been dancing with your sister for an hour. Where were you?"

"Detention," I said, and both Erma and Sissy went, "*Ooooooooh.*" "Listen, Sissy," I continued, "I can't dance tonight."

"Coach Abel said having a sore bum is no excuse to get out of dancing," she said. "Now come on." She held out her hands.

"I have homework," I said.

"No, you don't. I have all the same classes you do."

"It's extra credit. It's going to take me forever. Sorry."

"Thomas . . ." Erma warned, but I'd already turned and sprinted upstairs to my bedroom, where I dropped my backpack and grabbed my jacket. This time I wasn't even inventing excuses. Chip and I had called an emergency meeting at Pettigrew Park.

7

Wesley, Flea, and Owen were all waiting for us when we arrived.

"What's this about?" Owen said, tapping on his laptop, as if he could somehow search the answer to his question without us even speaking.

"Yeah. I'm missing didgeridoo lessons, so this better be important," Flea said.

"And I was halfway through taking off my stage makeup," Wesley said, pointing to his single penciled-in evil-villain eyebrow.

I climbed up the slide and stood at the top, raising my fists. "This, gentlemen, is about a revolution!"

Chip cheered; everyone else blinked up at me.

"A what?" Flea asked.

"A revolution," Owen said. He adjusted the soup pot he was wearing on his head.

"What kind of revolution?" Flea asked. "Because I have to be home by dinner."

"Oh! I'll be a redcoat!" Wesley said. He cleared his throat, straightened up, and adopted a British accent. "Prepare to be fired upon!"

"Technically," Chip said, "they were called lobsterbacks. And did you know that Paul Revere never shouted 'The redcoats are coming' as he rode alone through the streets?

Not to mention, he was not alone. William Dawes and Samuel Prescott were with him, and they picked up many more riders along the way. And they much more likely said 'The regulars are out' or 'The regulars are on the move.' Only they didn't yell it, because they were trying to keep their warning quiet. So you see—"

"Chip," I said, interrupting him. "Do you mind?"

"Oh. Certainly. As you were saying."

"As I was saying, we are revolting!"

Chip snickered.

"What?"

Chip waved me off and snickered some more.

"What?"

Chip laughed harder, his glasses sliding down his nose.

"What, Chip, what?" I snapped.

He took a breath and wiped tears from under his eyes. "It's just that . . . you said we're revolting. And the first thing I thought was, 'Well, speak for yourself. I've showered today.'" He doubled over in laughter while we all stood there and stared at him. Owen snaked his fingers under the pot and scratched his head. "Don't you get it?" Chip said between guffaws. "'We're revolting!' It's a double entendre." We flicked glances at one another. Wesley shrugged. Flea made the "cuckoo" motion at his temple with his finger. Chip, red-faced and breathless, straightened. "You know, double entendre.

Revolting, as in coming together in rebellion, or revolting as in disgusting. You said we're revolting, and—"

"Are you done?"

He giggled, hiccupped, and sniffed. "Quite." But the serious look on his face wavered, as if he could burst into giggles again at any moment.

A random little kid yanked on my pant leg and pointed at the slide. I slid down so he could go. No matter where you were in life, you could always count on some random little kid to make you have to move.

"If the interruptions are done . . ." I pointedly glared at Chip, who pressed his lips together, barely holding in another laughing fit. "We are going to rise up against Mr. Smith."

"Rise up against him? How?" Owen asked.

"I'm pretty sure my mom wouldn't want me rising up against things," Flea added.

"Not things," I said. "People. Or person. Ow." The little kid had slid down the slide and smacked into me, feetfirst. I rubbed the back of my knee.

"I don't know, Thomas," Wesley said. "I mean, if I get in trouble, it could hurt my chances of getting the lead in the spring musical. And you know what the spring musical is, don't you? *Grease*! And you know I'm a perfect Danny." He flipped pretend hair back and gave a cocky laugh.

"More like Sandy," Owen said. Wesley shoved him, and he fell backward into the little kids' sandpit, laughing.

"You guys. You won't get into trouble. You'll be making a difference. You'll be organizing a movement. Standing up for what you believe in. Isn't that what your parents want you to do?"

"It's just . . . the whole Heirmauser-head thing," Wesley said.

"I was a hero," I said.

"But first you got into a lot of trouble," Flea said.

"Like, a lot," Owen agreed.

"But don't you want to get rid of Mr. Smith? He's so . . . normal."

"Yeah, of course," Wesley said. "But guys like Mr. Smith don't last long at Pennybaker. He'll go away."

"And Mr. Faboo will still be gone," I said, "because we never bothered to figure out why."

"Sorry, Thomas." Flea grabbed Owen's wrist to get a look at his watch. "My parents pretty much want me to stay out of trouble and get into a good college with a solid didgeridoo program. Speaking of, I think I can still make the end of my lesson if I hurry." He walked along the balance beam on his way out.

Owen stood and brushed off the back of his pants. "Yeah, Thomas. I really have too many clubs right now, anyway. Robotics club, gaming club, coding club, Future Hackers of America . . ."

"No, you're not getting it. This isn't a club."

But Owen was sauntering away, continuing to list all his extracurricular activities as he went. "Architecture and engineering club, cupcake club . . ."

"Can you believe those guys?" I said to Wesley and Chip.

"Tell you what, pardner," Wesley said in a cowboy drawl. "If'n you need someone to rustle you up some beans for yer club meetins, I'm yer feller."

"There won't be any club meetings, because it's not a . . . Oh, forget it."

Wesley wandered off, singing a song about drive-ins.

I groaned and stomped to the merry-go-round. I plopped down—grimacing as my bruised rear end panged—and dug my toes into the dirt to keep it from spinning. Chip sat next to me.

"So I suppose this makes me vice president of this revolution club," he said. He saluted me. "I'm ready for the job, sir. I should go home and change into my leadership socks."

"Chip, it's not a club. It's a mission to find Mr. Faboo and get him back to Pennybaker School. He has to be out there somewhere. And there must be something keeping him away from school. Maybe we can help him out."

Chip's brow furrowed, and then he stuck his finger up in an "aha" pose. "So it's not a club!"

"That's what I've been saying."

"And it's not a revolution, really, either."

I shrugged. "Revolution just sounded cool. Like there

might be guts involved or something. Besides, it doesn't matter what it is if nobody is willing to help me."

"I'm willing to help you."

"Us. I meant nobody is willing to help us." Not really true—mostly because the Chip half of us was totally unhelpful.

Chip stood and paced back and forth in front of me, scratching his chin. "Maybe they don't want to help because you called it a revolution when it is not strictly a revolution. It's more of a . . ."

"Mystery," I finished for him.

He stopped abruptly, his whole body tense with excitement. "Exactly!" He grabbed the merry-go-round and gave it a mighty shove. Which, with Chip's size, meant it inched slowly in a half circle. I used my toes to bring me back to facing him. "And you know what we're good at?"

"What?"

He sat next to me and slung an arm around my shoulder. "Solving mysteries."

"You know what, Chip? You're right," I said. "Who needs those other guys anyway? We've got this."

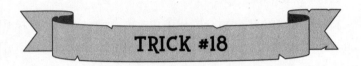

TRICK #18

THE PRAIRIEBALL PASS

So I didn't have a revolution to lead, but I had a mystery to solve, and a partner to help me solve it. If you could call Chip a partner and his help actual help. Both were iffy, especially if an interesting bug or flower or hat or shoe or just about anything at all happened to grab his attention.

But Chip was better than nobody. The important thing was finding Mr. Faboo and getting our school back to normal.

Or whatever passed for normal at our school. Which was not at all normal.

So getting our school back to not at all normal, but in a better not-at-all-normal way than the not-at-all-normal way it had been recently.

Chip promised to find out what the History-Lovers Society was doing, and I went home to sit on a pillow and work on another magic trick that might get me out of ballroom dancing so I could focus on solving the mystery.

Sissy Cork was the last person I wanted to see still at my house, now at my kitchen table, squaring up for an arm wrestling match with Grandma Jo. A mound of candy sat on the table between them. Dad stood next to them, a baseball cap on backward and a whistle dangling from his mouth. He was bent at the waist to get eye-to-elbow with Sissy and Grandma Jo.

The minute my eyes landed on Sissy, I tried to back out of the room, but it was too late. Erma had spotted me.

"It's about time," she said. "Sissy's been waiting here ever since you left."

"And she's robbed me blind," Grandma Jo added, rolling up her sleeve. "I'm completely out of butterscotch."

"I'll leave you to it," I said, trying again to get away.

Erma sidestepped so she was blocking the door. "You are going to dance whether you like it or not. Come on, Sissy."

Sissy started to get up, but Grandma Jo grabbed her wrist and pulled her back down. "Oh, no you don't, sister. You've got to give me a chance to win back the caramels at least."

Dad blew the whistle and grabbed his own wrist with his other hand. "Foul!" he called out one side of his mouth. "Illegal clutch of the wrist."

"Oh, it's okay," Sissy said, pushing the mound of candy across the table. "You can have it all back."

"Not the one you ate," Grandma Jo grumped. "Cheater."

"Grandma!" Erma said. "Let's go." She grabbed Sissy's hand with one of hers and my hand with the other. "You're not getting away this time." She pulled us both out of the room.

Dad's whistle sounded. "Forfeit!"

"Nobody likes a quitter!" Grandma Jo called to our backs.

<hr/>

"Okay, so the first step to good dancing is posture," Erma said. Sissy stood stiff as a board. A very angry board, glaring at me. Erma placed her hand on my back and shoved. I stumbled forward.

"Hey!"

"Straighten up!" she said, clapping her hands with every syllable. I straightened. "And put your shoulders back." I did so. "Chin!" she barked. I lifted my chin.

"I can see up your nose now," Sissy said.

I slumped. My stomach started up. "Erma, do we have to—"

"Posture!" Erma said, shoving my back again.

"Ouch! I have a bruise."

"Stop whining. There is no whining in dance." She was really pushing my limits. "Hands, please." Sissy held up her hands, and Erma grabbed mine and placed one on Sissy's back and the other in her hand. "Close your fingers, Thomas." I didn't want to, but I did it, just to make her quiet. "Get a little closer." We closed the gap between us by about a centimeter. "Good. Now, Thomas, you're going to step forward with this leg, and Sissy, you're going to step backward with that one. I'll clap out the beat. Ready?" I wasn't, but I figured the quicker I got this over with, the quicker I could be put out of my misery. "Okay, one-two-three-four-one-two-three-four-one—"

A knock on the front door interrupted us. I dropped Sissy's hand and practically bolted out of the room, thinking I owed whoever was on the other side of the door a candy bar or a gold star or a pony.

Of course, it was Chip.

"I've got a new plan," he said the minute I opened the door.

"Already?"

"Thomas," Erma called.

"Sorry, I've got to take care of this," I said over my shoulder, and prodded Chip out of my way and off the porch. "Your house," I said.

The best thing about Chip's house was that there was no Erma there. And, right now, no Sissy Cork, either. The second best thing about Chip's house was that the basement had an old-timey pinball machine, and Chip didn't mind if I played it for as long as I wanted.

"So what's the plan?" I asked, grabbing a coin from Chip's cup of quarters and plugging it into the machine. It instantly came to life with a bunch of dings and whistles.

"You know, you're going to have to dance at some point," he said, sidling up next to me. He bumped the machine with his hip, sending the little metal ball right into a jackpot hole.

"Not if I can help it," I said. "So far I've been pretty good at avoiding it."

"Not true," Chip said. "So far you've gotten lucky. Pretty soon Sissy is going to start demanding it."

"I'll figure out my strategy then," I said. I missed the ball, and it rolled into the gutter behind my flippers. "Darn it."

"It's not really all that bad. It's kind of fun, actually."

"Says you," I said.

"Anyone can dance. You want me to show you?" He bumped the machine again, and the ball fell back into the jackpot hole. Chip was really good at being the kind of friend who helps people get a jackpot when they need one.

"No. I want you to tell me what your new lead for find-ing Mr. Faboo is," I said.

"The Prairie High Pioneers!" he said, sticking his finger in the air.

I lost my last ball, and the machine shut down. I reached for another quarter. "What's that?"

"What's what?"

"The Prairie High Pioneers."

"A basketball team, of course," he said. "It being basketball season and all."

I tossed and caught the new quarter a few times. "So what does this basketball team have to do with your plans?"

"A little research turned up a very tasty little factoid about our absent educator."

I squinted at him. "Are you talking about something to eat?" I tossed the quarter. It bounced off Chip's palm and rolled under the machine.

"I'm talking about finding Mr. Faboo." He dropped and crawled under the machine to retrieve the coin, but I simply dug a new one out of the cup. Chip crawled out. A spiderweb was stuck to his hair. "Turns out he has a bit of extra employment on the side."

"He's a coach?"

"Nope. He's a mascot."

I stopped, the flipper frozen in the up position. The ball whizzed by and thunked into the gutter again. "Huh?"

"He's a pioneer," he clarified. "Well, an imaginary pioneer. He dresses in costume and dances around on the court to entertain the crowd. Sometimes he dances with the cheerleaders or does little stunts. I've read that a mascot can even sometimes shoot T-shirts out of a gun. I'm having a hard time believing that a T-shirt would fit in a musket barrel, but—"

"I know what a mascot is, Chip," I said. The machine beeped at me, letting me know that it was waiting, but I ignored it. Envisioning Mr. Faboo dancing around a basketball court and leading cheers was enough for my brain to handle at once.

"Well, he does enjoy dressing up," I said, remembering the brown pants and suspenders that Mr. Faboo wore when we talked about the Oregon Trail. He'd mentioned that his dream was to someday own a covered wagon and live on salt meat. I didn't know what salt meat was, but it sounded to me like if picky Erma lived in pioneer times, she would probably starve to death.

"Indeed he does. And he must enjoy dancing, too. Perhaps even turning a cartwheel or two." Chip tapped his chin. "I wonder if he would like to borrow my cartwheel socks."

I couldn't imagine Mr. Faboo dancing, but I supposed anything was possible.

"So what's your plan? Go to a Prairie High basketball game?"

"Yes." Chip beamed.

"And then get to Mr. Faboo?"

"Yes," he said again.

"How?"

"That's the brilliant part of my plan," he said. "We can't expect to be allowed down onto the court as two fans, although I did consider faking an illness or perhaps telling the gatekeepers that we're cousins of the point guard—but I decided there's no reason to test karma with deceit. I know a lot of people don't believe in karma. In fact, many people believe that—"

"Chip! Focus!" I said, placing my palms on his cheeks and forcing him to look at me. He dropped the quarter he'd been holding, and it rolled back under the pinball machine.

"Yes, of course. Focused," he said, only I was kind of squishing his cheeks a little, so it sounded like, "Yesh, of courshe. Focushed."

I let go of his cheeks, brushed off his shoulders, and very slowly, very softly asked, "How are we going to get to Mr. Faboo?"

"Breeches," he said with confidence.

"Excuse me?"

"I've already asked, and my mom will take us to Prairie High. We're going to dress up and pretend to be spirit leaders. It's a thing. I looked it up. Apparently, a spirit leader is one who engages the audience—"

"Crowd," I corrected.

"Yes, crowd. Engages the crowd in recitation of various plaudits perpetuated by the cheerleaders."

"I know what a spirit leader does—he gets the crowd to go crazy when the team does cool stuff."

"Exactly as I said."

I didn't know if that was exactly what he'd said, but I

was too busy thinking Chip's plan through to argue with him. Besides, he pretty much always won arguments about vocabulary.

"So if I understand you correctly, we're going to dress up as pioneers, go to the Prairie High basketball game, and pretend to be spirit leaders."

"Correct."

This was the dumbest plan I'd heard in a long time. Or maybe just since our last dumb plan, which was also pretty dumb. Chip and I sort of specialized in dumb plans. I thought it over. Crashing a high school basketball game was a bold move.

But it was still better than sitting in detention with boring Mr. Smith.

"Will I have to wear pantyhose?" I asked.

"Of course not."

"Then I'm in."

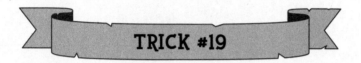

TRICK #19

THE RACING BOUQUET WAND

A *click* and a *whoosh* noise woke me up. I blinked at the clock. It was two in the morning. It took me a minute to realize that once again I was cold, and that the noise that had awakened me was the trick I'd planted in my window before I went to bed. I'd collapsed my flower cane and hooked the locking mechanism to the lock on the window using clear thread. When the window was opened, it would unlock the cane, and poof! There would be a beautiful bouquet of feather flowers.

And hopefully Grandma Jo.

But when I sat up, there was no Grandma Jo—only the flowers, dangling from the window shade, something stuck to the end of them.

Quickly, I scrambled out of bed and examined the

bouquet. It was sticking right through the center of a piece
of paper. I pulled the paper off.

It had a number on it—308—and the words "Boone County
Speedway" written across the top, with a black-and-white
checkered flag waving above them.

Boone County Speedway, number 308?

"A race car number?" I asked aloud. As if in response, an
engine revved outside. I leaned out the window just in time
to see a shadowy figure tiptoeing out to a slick-looking car,

planting a helmet on its head as it moved along. The figure got into the car and it peeled out, leaving a small cloud of smoke and the rumble of loud rock and roll music behind.

I closed the window and went back to bed, clutching the paper with the number to my chest.

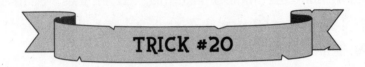

TRICK #20

PICK A DRESS, ANY DRESS

The next day at school, Chip and I invited Wesley and the others to join us in Prairie City that evening, but each of them had an excuse.

I have rehearsal.

I have practice.

I have to babysit.

I have to make dinner for my cat's birthday.

All the excuses boiled down to one thing—they didn't want to go. Except maybe the cat one. I was pretty sure that was real.

"So, Mom," I said when I got home from school, "would it be okay if I went to a basketball game tonight?"

Mom was kneeling, the top half of her inside the hall closet, picking up shoes, flipping them over to examine them, and putting them back down. A hunk of hair hung down over her face, and she looked kind of sweaty.

"I didn't know Pennybaker had a basketball team," she said, her voice coming out all closety.

"We don't. It's at Prairie High School."

She sat back on her heels and blew the hair out of her eyes. "Huh?"

"It's a Prairie High School game," I repeated.

"Oh, Thomas, I don't know. A high school game? You know the kind of things that could go on at a high school game."

Actually, I didn't. Mom had never let me have a High School Adventure before, mostly because she was worried that a High School Adventure would be a Horrible Things Happen to Thomas Adventure and she would maybe have to bail me out of jail or something.

"Mom, I'll be with Chip," I said.

"Oh." She thought about it, blew the hair out of her face again, and leaned back inside. "Well, I suppose it's okay, then."

Mom loved Chip. She would pretty much let me go to a chainsaw-sharpening convention wearing a shirt made of broken glass and eating a dead-fly sandwich made by a guy with the flu as long as Chip was going to be with me. I tried not to take it personally, mostly because I was afraid that taking it personally would give her a reason to think things over and maybe change her mind.

"Thanks!" I said, and started to walk away. Then it occurred to me that she was studying the bottoms of shoes. I turned back. "Hey, Mom?"

"Yes, Thomas," she said in her closety voice again, sounding a little aggravated.

"What are you doing?"

She sat back on her heels, a shoe in each hand. They were both Grandma Jo's shoes—one from a pair that Grandma Jo wore when she had to go to a funeral or a fancy dinner like normal grandmas, and one from a pair that I once saw her wear to an archery lesson.

"Checking shoes," she said, as if that made total sense. I must have made a face that told her it didn't make total sense at all, because she rolled her eyes, let out an exasperated breath, and held the soles of the shoes up for me to see. "I'm checking the bottoms of your grandmother's shoes to see if any of them have fresh dirt on the bottom."

"Why?"

Mom leaned toward me. If she was a cartoon, her eyes would have had swirls in them. "Because she's up to something, I just know it. And she's not doing it barefoot."

I didn't know why Mom would assume that Grandma Jo wouldn't get into an adventure while barefoot.

Mom squinted one eye at me in her best I'm Getting to the Bottom of This Adventure look. "You don't know anything about what she might be up to, do you, Thomas?"

I remembered the figure I'd seen in the middle of the night, hurrying away from my window and hopping into the race car. That person was definitely wearing shoes. Boots, actually. But I didn't think it was a good time to share that with Mom. Mostly because I was having fun trying to catch Grandma Jo in the act, and if Mom shut Grandma Jo down, she would be shutting me down, too.

"Nope."

She sagged a little, then bent back into the closet. "Have a good time at the game. And be careful. And eat something before you go!"

I threw on my jacket, raced into the kitchen, and stuck a hot dog in the microwave. Grandma Jo was sitting in front of the TV playing solitaire again. While my hot dog cooked, I crept into the living room.

"Well, hello, Thomas," Grandma Jo said, laying down a two of clubs. "Going out tonight?"

I locked my eyes on hers. "Are you?"

She gathered the cards together and shuffled them, then began laying them out again. "Nope, can't say that I am. Just watching a little TV here." She gestured to the television. I leaned forward to see what she was watching. Tiny cars roared around a racetrack.

"Car races?" I said, more to myself than to her, but before she could respond, Erma bounced into the room.

"There you are! Don't go anywhere," she said.

The microwave beeped, and I went to it. "I'm going to a basketball game with Chip," I said over my shoulder.

"But you can't," she said, following me.

"Mom said I could."

"But you can't," she repeated. "Sissy's coming over."

I grabbed a slice of bread and quickly wrapped it around my hot dog. I definitely needed to get out of there before Sissy arrived. "Sorry," I said. I took a huge bite out of my hot dog and hurried toward the front door. "Gotta go." Only my mouth was full, so it sounded like, "Gorra gor."

"You haven't even learned your dance at all yet. Thomas! Mom!"

I didn't look back; I just lunged out the front door before my stomach started in again.

⁊

Chip was standing at the top of his steps, looking way too uneasy for everything to be okay.

"What?" I asked, slowing with every step. With Chip, you never knew whether he looked uneasy because he had accidentally tromped on an anthill and was feeling guilty for decimating an entire ant universe or because something was really wrong.

"Don't get mad," he said.

So something was really wrong.

"What?" I asked again, swallowing the last of my hot dog, which suddenly didn't want to go down. "Are we not going? Because if we aren't, I have to lay low over here for a little while. I'll teach you how to burn a dollar bill without actually burning it." Chip was always bribe-able with the promise of learning a magic trick.

"No, no, we're going," he said. "It's just . . . Follow me."

It was never good when Chip was talking like a normal kid. I didn't want to, but I followed him inside his house and up to his bedroom, where a mess of clothes was scattered on his bed. Nothing really looked that out of the ordinary. Of course, that was mostly because Chip didn't do ordinary, so *everything* looked out of the ordinary. It made sense in a converse sort of way.

"Okay, so what's the deal?" I asked.

He went to the bed, picked up a wad of clothes, and held it up, letting it unfurl in front of him. It was a long pink dress with little white flowers on it.

"A dress?" I still didn't understand what the problem was, until he dropped it and shook out a second, blue, dress. That one had ruffles on the shoulders. "Oh no." I shook my head. "No, no, no."

"Just bear with me," he said, dropping the blue dress and coming toward me, arms outstretched as if to stop me from running.

"No way, Chip. When you said pioneer clothes, I thought you meant man clothes."

"I did," he said. "But unfortunately, the only garb I was able to secure on such short notice is of the feminine variety."

I pointed in his face. "That means you want us to dress like girls."

"No, I don't *want* us to. It just happens that we have no choice in the matter."

"Correction. *You* have no choice in the matter. I'm not putting that on." I kicked at the pink dress.

"Of course not, of course not!" he said, bending to pick up the two dresses. "I never expected you to." He pressed the blue dress against my chest. "Pink is a much more suitable match to my skin color than to yours."

"I'll just wear this," I said, pointing at my jeans, refusing to take the dress.

"And get turned away by security. You will never pass as a pioneer in that ridiculous getup."

I glanced down at my "ridiculous getup," which just happened to be my normal clothes. This from the guy holding a Laura Ingalls Wilder outfit.

"Come on, Thomas. It's for an hour at most. Don't you want to solve the Great Faboo Mystery?"

"The what?"

"The Mystery of the Disappearance of Faboo."

"No. Chip. Don't do that."

"Do what?"

"Title our . . . whatever this is."

"It's a mystery. You said so yourself."

"I meant more of a . . . curiosity."

"The Mystery of the Lost Professor."

"No."

"The Skedaddled Scholar?"

"Absolutely not."

He held the dress toward me again. I stared at it. "It's just fabric," he said. "We have to do this if we want to get onto that court."

I stared at the blue dress for a few seconds longer and then sighed and snatched the garment out of his hands. "Fine. But there better be a hat in there somewhere, because we are never going to pass for girls."

"Fear not!" he said, poking one finger to the sky. He practically dove onto his bed and came up with something white and frilly.

"What is . . ."

He wrapped the white frilly thing over his head and tied it with a big bow under his chin.

"Bonnets!" he crowed. As if that was a good thing.

We were silent as we climbed into our dresses and aprons and bonnets. Chip insisted that we roll our pant legs up to our knees and put on lace-up boots that made my feet feel like they were being strangled. *"For authenticity,"* he'd said.

Finally, we stood side by side in the mirror, looking at ourselves.

"Your dress fits better," I said, plucking at my waist. "Mine is all baggy here." I yanked up the dress and studied my feet. "And my shoes don't match at all. I should be wearing those cream-colored ones, and you should be wearing these . . ." I trailed off as I realized what I was saying. "Come on. Let's go."

We went downstairs and found Chip's mom, who was wearing sporty jeans and a sweatshirt. She squealed with delight when she saw us, and immediately ran for her camera. I gave Chip a death glare while she was gone.

"Aren't you two just the cutest little things?" she said, snapping away. "Oh, Thomas. Your shoes are just adorable." Great. Exactly what I wanted to be: *the cutest* and *adorable*— and caught on camera for the whole world to see.

After what seemed like nine hundred thousand photos, she finally put her camera away and shouldered her purse.

"Should we go?"

"Absolutely!" Chip said, sounding way too cheerful for a guy who was about to have to sit with his knees together for a whole car ride.

Chip sang a bunch of goofy songs about valleys and starlight and some dog named Tray, and for a while it felt like Prairie High was on the other side of the earth rather than just on the other side of town.

"Why don't you sing something normal?" I asked as we pulled onto the highway.

"This is normal for the eighteen hundreds. I figure if we're going to act the part, we might as well be authentic."

I picked up a handful of skirt and waved it at him. "This isn't authentic enough for you?"

He rubbed the fabric between his finger and thumb. "Well, technically, not really. This dress is made of cotton, and it really should be wool or linen, as those were the pre-dominant textiles available at the time." I gave him a look. He shrugged. "What? You asked."

"No, I was not asking about what type of textures dresses were made of in the eighteen hundreds."

"Textiles," he said.

"What?"

"Textiles," he repeated. "You said 'textures,' and while it's true that varying textiles do have varying textures, the word you were searching for was definitely 'textiles.'"

I stared at him, then turned to look out the window.

Before he could get to the end of a song about firelight, we pulled into the Prairie High School parking lot. And it was only then that it really sank in that I was about to walk into a high school full of rowdy teenagers while wearing a floor-length dress and a bonnet. I stared out the window in horror as Chip bounded from the car.

"Something wrong, Thomas?" Mrs. Mason asked.

"N-no," I said, although I couldn't get my fingers to wrap around the door handle.

"I'll be back in a couple of hours," she said cheerfully. Too cheerfully. I still didn't move. "So . . ."

"Yeah," I said. "Actually, I think I hear my mom call—"

I didn't get to finish, because Chip had come to my side and whipped open the door. He curtsied, and three girls burst into giggles.

"Go on, boys," Mrs. Mason said, and I could see Chip was about to curtsy again, so I swallowed and slid out of the car to stop him. It didn't work. He waited until I was standing next to him, shut the door, curtsied again, and said in a high-pitched girl voice, "Let's go, Mabel."

"No," I said through clenched teeth. "Don't do that, or I will get back in that car and go home."

Mrs. Mason pulled away from the curb. I watched as she drove out of the parking lot, leaving Chip and me and our fancy dresses behind.

"Do you prefer Martha?" he asked. I started walking. "Minnie?" he asked to my back. I continued forward, eyes pointed straight ahead so I wouldn't see the amused looks on the faces of the teenagers we passed. "Wait. Thomas," Chip said when we reached the front door.

"What?"

"I have a title for our mission."

"I told you not to title it."

He spread his hands out, as if he were reading from a sign. "The Perplexing Case of the Teacher Who Is History. Get it? He's a history teacher, and . . . You get it, right?"

Without a word, I pulled open the door and walked into the school.

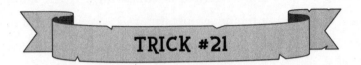

TRICK #21

THE EMBARRASSMENT EFFECT

Inside, the school was a bustle of noise and movement. Every time I heard a laugh, I was convinced it was directed at me. I never thought I would wish for breeches and suspenders, but I did.

I pulled Chip into a dark hallway, slipping past the accordion gate blocking it off for the night. I could hear the echo of a whistle blowing in the distance, along with the thud of a bouncing basketball.

"Where are we supposed to go?" I hissed.

"How would I know?" Chip asked, scratching beneath his bonnet.

"It was your plan," I said. "I figured you had it all mapped out."

He shook his head. "Part of the fun of a mission is learning things along the way with and about your partner. For example, while perusing the halls of Prairie High, I might discover that you are allergic to asparagus but eat it anyway, and you might discover that I have a toothpick collection."

"You have a toothpick collection?"

"No, but if I did, you might discover that during our mission here tonight. See?"

No, I totally didn't see, but how does someone argue with that kind of logic? "Come on," I said. I grabbed his sleeve and pulled him behind me as I plunged down a shadowy stairwell, the sounds of the gym getting farther away.

"Where are we going?"

"I don't know, but anywhere is better than standing around in flowery dresses in front of a bunch of high schoolers. Come on."

We got to the bottom of the staircase and turned right. The hallway was even darker than the stairwell, but I had a hunch that if we followed it, we would come up on the other side of the field house. Maybe there would be fewer people on that side.

Sure enough, there was another stairwell at the other end of the hall, and we raced up, both of us hiking our skirts so we didn't trip over them. I was starting to understand why Grandma Jo almost never wore dresses: it was really hard to accomplish anything in one. The crowd noise got louder again as we neared the top of the stairs, but it wasn't as loud as before. We craned our necks, straining to look left and right.

A custodian at the far end of the hallway was pushing a trash can away from us, toward a door.

"It's clear," I whispered. We crept the rest of the way up and peered through the small windows on the field house doors. The game was in full swing; it was only a minute or so before halftime. "Do you see him?" I asked.

"No," Chip said. "Oh, wait. There he is!" He pointed. Up in the stands, about four rows from the top, a man in brown pants and a vest, very much like the Pennybaker uniform, danced in the aisle, shaking his hips wildly. He had a huge fuzzy beard and a wide-brimmed hat. "He's awfully far away," Chip said.

"Yeah. Maybe we can wait for him in the locker room."

"Good idea."

We each went separate ways, looking for a locker room door. I was just about to give up and turn around when Chip whistled at me. I turned back to see him holding open a door and pointing inside.

"Good work, Chip," I said, jogging to catch up with him. We slipped through.

"Thank goodness," Chip said. "I've had to go since we left the house." He disappeared into a stall.

But something was weird about this locker room. I couldn't quite pinpoint it.

"Hurry up," I said. "We don't want to miss him if he comes in after halftime."

"Okay, okay, hold your horses," Chip said. He sounded like he was wrestling with a feisty bear in there. "Corsets aren't easy to undo, you know."

"You're wearing a corset?" I knew exactly what a corset was. Grandma Jo had one, and she called it a girdle.

"You're not?" He sighed. "I told you, Thomas, I wanted to be as authentic as possible. I laid yours out on the bed next to your dress. We need to go home now and get it."

"I don't think so," I said, but the words came out soft and slow as I scanned the room. It was gradually dawning on me what was weird about this locker room. "Hey, Chip?"

"Huh?"

"Is there a urinal inside that stall, by chance?"

He laughed. "Why would there be a urinal inside a stall?"

My eyes landed on a little sparkly pink bag someone had left on the edge of the sink. I picked it up. "Because there isn't one out here." The bag was open a little bit, and inside I could see a bunch of little tubes and bottles and brushes. A makeup bag.

The toilet flushed, and there was more fumbling and bumping inside the stall, and then the door opened and Chip came out. "What?"

I held the bag toward him. "Chip, I think we're in the—"

Voices roared into the room as the door flew open and a whole bunch of girls poured into the locker room. They were giggling and talking all at the same time, just like girls always did, and they were wearing much shorter versions of the dresses we were wearing.

"Oh, no," I said. "Hide."

I reached for Chip's arm, but I was too late. One of the cheerleaders had spotted us. "Hey," she said. "What are you doing in here?"

"It was a mistake," I said, or at least I thought I said, but my voice was really small and scared, because I was pretty sure I was about to get creamed by a whole bunch of girl pioneers.

"You missed the entire first half," she said, paying no attention to what I'd said. I ducked my head so she couldn't see my face under the bonnet. I elbowed Chip, and he did the same.

"Sorry," I said, raising the pitch of my voice, hoping I sounded like a girl. While also hating it a little that it was so easy for me to sound like a girl.

She thrust her hand into the glittery bag and pulled out a tube of lipstick. She smeared it on her lips, gave her hair a quick fluff, and said to her reflection in the mirror, "Ready? Okay. The least you can do is get out there for the halftime show. We go on in thirty seconds."

Sure enough, all the other girls were rushing around, grabbing new pom-poms out of their lockers and retying their bootlaces.

"Why are their dresses so long?" one of them asked when we walked by.

"New girls," someone answered her. "I think they're from private school."

Well, at least they had that much right.

"They look ridiculous," the first girl said. She didn't know how right she really was. "We need to get them real uniforms."

"No time," said the girl ushering us out of the locker room.

"Well, at least put them in the back row," another girl said.

"Fine, whatever. I assume you two know the routine? Coach Danner has caught you up?" She thrust pom-poms at us.

I was frantically searching my brain for an answer that would get us out of having to go on, when Chip said, "Sure we do!" I tried to shoot him a death glare, but my bonnet was flopping too low to catch his eye.

There was a muffled boom of music starting, and the girls all jumped into frantic motion.

"Let's go, let's go, let's go," one of them chanted while pushing past us.

"New girls! Just try to keep up!" shouted the one shoving us toward the door.

"Ready? Okay!" they screamed in unison, and then yanked open the door and flooded out, spitting us into the bright lights of the field house.

They rushed into four neat lines. I tripped forward as each one raced past me, pom-poms on hips, bonnet ties bouncing on their backs.

"Get in line," one spat through clenched teeth and a forced smile.

"Let's get out of here," I said, turning to Chip—only Chip wasn't there. I spun in a circle. There he was, lined up with the girls, holding his pom-poms proudly.

I barely had time to register what he was doing when the line shifted, and I got shoved forward.

"Step ball change," the clenched-teeth girl growled. "Kick, kick, kick, drop."

I stood awkwardly as all the girls—and Chip, who was a surprisingly fast learner—step-ball-changed and kicked and dropped around me. The music changed, and so did the formation, the lines closing in to form three big circles. The lights dimmed as I stutter-stepped, trying to keep up, certain that I would actually drop dead of embarrassment.

"Chip," I tried every time I passed him, but he didn't seem to hear me. "Chip!"

"This way," the clenched-teeth girl said, pushing my shoulder toward the middle of a circle. "You're the smallest, so you're going to cupie."

"I'm going to what?"

"Cupie," she repeated, but I didn't even have time to ask what that was before I was grabbed and lifted up by the waist. Two girls palmed the soles of my feet and hoisted me to shoulder height.

"Whoa, whoa, whoa!" I shouted, grabbing at their shoulders with my hands.

"Just relax. You're messing it up," the girl shouted into my ear. "Straighten your legs."

"No way."

"Let. Go. Of. Them. And. Straighten."

I whimpered.

"Look. Your friend is doing it."

I looked to my right and, sure enough, there was Chip, standing high and proud atop his cluster of cheerleaders, his arms in the air victoriously. Seriously, did the kid even have cupie socks?

"Do it!" the girl growled, and moved her hands from my waist to my ankles. She counted—"Five, six, seven, eight"—and the next thing I knew, I was teetering so high above the hard field house floor I might as well have been in an airplane. My arms wheeled out to my sides as I desperately tried to keep upright.

"Smile," the girl shouted.

Nope. No way. Who smiles on their way to certain death?

"Okay, five, six, seven, eight!" she cried, and the next thing I knew, I was being launched into the air. "Pike, pike!" she was shouting.

But I didn't pike. Instead, I flailed. And screamed. And apparently, flailing and screaming throws off a cupie formation. In fact, when you flail and scream the specific words "I'm gonna puke!" it causes all the other girls in your formation to take two steps back. And instead of landing safely cradled in their arms—as I saw Chip do out of the corner of my eye—you land on the floor, on your back and on your bruised tailbone, so hard it knocks the wind out of you. Again. And you're so busy rolling around on the floor in agony, you don't even realize your dress has billowed up over your head, showing off your rolled-up boy jeans and your sweat socks poking out of a pair of old-fashioned lace-up boots.

When I finally got my breath back, I realized that the entire gym had gone quiet. I clawed my way out from under my dress and opened my eyes to find a circle of angry cheerleaders standing above me. And Chip. He leaned down so his face was sort of close to mine and whispered, "Technically, a pike is—"

"I know what a pike is," I snapped, sitting up. My back felt like it had been slapped. By a floor.

"You're a boy," one of the cheerleaders said, pointing out the obvious. I ripped off my bonnet and tossed it to the side. There was an audible gasp from the crowd. "You're both boys."

"They were in the girls' locker room," another cheerleader said, her voice coming way too close to a shriek for my comfort.

"We weren't trying to be," I said. "We were looking for someone."

A referee parted the circle and crouched over me. "You all right, son?" he asked. I nodded. He picked me up by my elbow. "Good. It's time for you to leave. You, too, Little Red Riding Hood."

"Technically, I'm wearing a bonnet, not a hood. And also my dress is pink, not red. And I'm not on my way to deliver baked goods to my grandmother. You should possibly consider brushing up on your fairy tales."

"Okay, Little Pink Riding Bonnet, how about you take your baked goods on out of here," the referee said, leading us across the field house floor.

"I don't have any baked goods," Chip said, and the referee might have thought he was being smart with him, but that was the kind of thing that really did mess with Chip. You were accurate or you were inaccurate. There wasn't a lot of in between.

We were deposited on the front walk of the school. I shrugged out of my dress and bonnet and tossed them on the ground next to my feet. Chip stayed in his, primly smoothing his skirt over his knees.

"Dresses are quite comfortable, don't you agree, Thomas?"

I stared at him.

"What?" he asked.

"Seriously? You have to ask what? We were just kicked

out of a high school basketball game, but not before making sure we completely humiliated ourselves. And we didn't even get anywhere close to Mr. Faboo."

"Oh. That." He thought for a moment, and then brightened. "I know what we can do."

"What?"

"Well, my mom won't be here until after the game is over. And the referee said we had to leave the game, but he didn't say we had to leave the school grounds. I propose we wait here for the game to be over and for Mr. Faboo to come out."

It was a pretty reasonable plan. So reasonable, in fact, some might say we should have started with it and forgotten all about the costumes and the spirit-leader thing. So we waited. And we waited. And we waited. Chip sang the periodic table song. And then sang it again backward. And again in French. And just when he asked if I'd like to hear him sing it in pig Latin while doing a handstand, the doors opened, and Prairie High fans began to stream out. I could tell by the way their heads hung low that the team hadn't won the game.

Chip and I slid around to the side of the building and peeked around the corner, watching for Mr. Faboo. Just when we thought he wouldn't be coming at all, the door opened and out he came, walking with the same referee who'd kicked us out.

"In three," Chip whispered. "One—"

But I didn't wait for him to finish. I darted out from behind the school and made a beeline for the pioneer.

"Caught you!" I yelled as I reached up to grab Mr. Faboo's fake beard. Only it didn't come off. And it wasn't fake. And the pioneer who yelled "*Ouch!*" and jumped back, rubbing his cheek, wasn't Mr. Faboo at all.

"What was that for?" he asked.

"I thought I told you two to leave," the referee said.

"Technically," Chip said, pointing one finger in the air as he slowly sauntered toward us, "you told us to leave the game. But there was no game going on out here."

"I should call the police," the referee said.

"Please don't," I said. "We didn't mean to hurt anyone. We were just looking for Mr. Faboo, and we thought the pioneer was him."

"Who?" the pioneer asked. He was still rubbing his cheek.

"Mr. Faboo. Our history teacher." I pointed to Chip. "He said Mr. Faboo is a mascot here."

The referee and the pioneer exchanged glances. "Oh," they said in unison. "Francis."

"Who?" Chip asked, at the same time that I said, "His name is Francis Faboo?"

"He's the *football* mascot," the pioneer said. "Football season's over. We won't see him again until August."

I gave Chip a death glare. "Football mascot?" I repeated.

Chip shrugged. "I thought every sport was the same." The one thing Chip wasn't smart about was sports—so why had I trusted him to lead us to Prairie High? Because I wasn't smart at remembering what going on adventures with Chip was like.

"So do you know where he is?" I asked.

The pioneer shook his head.

I could feel my shoulders sag. Mrs. Mason pulled up to the curb and gave a short honk. "Sorry I pulled your beard," I said. "And sorry I messed up the cupie," I said to the ref.

"Let's go, Thomas," Chip said.

I turned away from the pioneer and the referee. "And I'm sorry I ever listened to you," I said. But Chip either didn't hear me or didn't care.

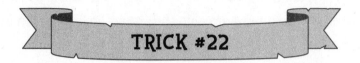

TRICK #22

THE TIME MACHINE PROPOSAL

Thanks to Boone County being a pretty small town, by the time we got to school the next day, pretty much everyone knew all about the Prairie High basketball game. Kids snickered when we walked by, and a couple of guys asked if their sisters could borrow some clothes from us.

It was humiliating, sure, but I was too busy trying to figure out a quick-change trick to worry about it.

I hadn't asked her yet, and I wasn't yet sure what I was going to use to bribe her into it, but I had this great idea that somehow Erma could be the one dancing with Sissy Cork, and make it look like it was me. The illusion was called Metamorphosis, and was created by the great Harry Houdini himself. Grandpa Rudy used to talk about Jonathan and Charlotte Pendragon, two magicians who were so quick at Metamorphosis, they got into the *Guinness Book of World Records*.

The way it worked was a magician would usually stuff himself into some kind of bag and then hop into a trunk, and his assistant would lock the trunk with a padlock. Then the assistant would jump up onto the trunk, hold a curtain over herself for a second or two, and out would pop the magician. Grandpa Rudy's videos of the Pendragons were really impressive. I'd never tried it before—mostly because I didn't have a trunk, other than Grandpa Rudy's magic trunk, which kind of smelled a little, so I didn't love the idea of being locked inside it—but surely there had to be a way to figure out how to use it to get out of dancing.

"Hey, look, it's our famous cheerleader," Colton cried when I walked into the lunchroom that day. "Show us how to do the splits, Thomas."

"Do a backflip!" Buckley added.

"Yeah, yeah, whatever," I mumbled, slouching up to the table with my tray. I sat very gingerly. Chip occupied the space between the other two, happily eating his yogurt parfait. He didn't seem to mind being teased at all.

"So, Thomas," Chip said after I got settled. "I have another lead."

"Oh, really?" I asked, taking a big bite out of my burger. "I can't wait to hear how I'm going to be humiliated next."

"Oh, c'mon dere," Wesley said, trying on his Southern voice to practice for his *Oklahoma* audition. "It cain't be all dat bad now, cain it?" He pretended to lob a loogie into a spittoon.

"I don't know, Wesley. You try going out in public in a dress and tell me how bad it is."

"Edna Turnblad," he said in what I'd heard him refer to as his Baltimore voice. I'd forgotten that he'd played the role of the main character's mother in *Hairspray* last summer. "One of my best roles."

"Actually," Chip said, "I was thinking maybe all of you fellows would like to join us this time."

Buckley and Colton burst out laughing. "Not likely."

"Depends," Flea said, settling onto the bench next to me. His didgeridoo slid over to the side and bonked me on the head. I barely even noticed. It was sort of understood that if you were friends with Flea, you were going to get bonked with his didgeridoo pretty much every day. "Where are you going?"

Chip fussily dabbed the corners of his mouth with his napkin, carefully laid it on his tray, and leaned forward. "Rumor among those in the History-Lovers Society is Mr. Faboo is the blacksmith out at Old Midwest Town on the weekends."

"Old Midwest Town?" Owen asked. "What's that?"

"The year is 1855, and our wagons have happed across a thriving town," Chip started, spreading his hands as if to paint the picture of Old Midwest Town. "A church stands high and proud in the center." His hands indicated a very tall church. "A one-room schoolhouse employs the young daughter of the colonel, who lives over here"—we all followed his hands—"in this mansion."

"Whoa, a mansion?" Flea breathed.

"Well, a three-room house, anyway. With two whole stories. Might as well have been a mansion."

"Is Mr. Faboo the colonel?" Flea asked.

"No, dummy, he's the blacksmith. Weren't you listening?" Colton tossed a wadded-up napkin at Flea; it bounced off his forehead and into his chili. He made a face as he plucked it out.

"Right next to the trading post," Chip said.

I had been to Old Midwest Town before, but it had been a long time, and I couldn't really remember it. Had Mr. Faboo been the blacksmith when I was there? It was totally possible. "What does he do all day?" I asked.

Chip shrugged. "Makes horseshoes and stuff. And talks about what it was like to be a blacksmith in 1855."

"So we're just going to go out to this place and pretend we need horseshoes or something?" Colton asked.

"There's a festival," Chip said. "It's going on all weekend. We can ride our bikes there on Saturday."

"I don't know," I said. "Where did you hear about—"

"We're in!" Wesley interrupted.

"We are?"

He nodded. "It'll give me awl kindsa practice with my drawl."

I had no idea what he was saying, but I could roughly translate it to: character, character, blah blah, rehearsal.

"I don't know," I said. "Every time I listen to one of Chip's—"

"No, Wesley's right. I think it's a good idea," Owen said. He turned his laptop around so we could see a photo of the town. Sure enough, right out front, beaming for all the world to see, was a blacksmith. His face was smudged with soot and he was kind of squinting into the sun, so it was hard to tell exactly who it was, but it definitely could have been Mr. Faboo.

"Whoa. Wait a minute. I thought you guys didn't want to be in my revolution," I said.

"But Chip makes this sound fun," Wesley said.

"Yeah, it's not really a revolution. It's a festival. And they probably have apple cider and homemade doughnuts and stuff," Owen added.

I didn't care if they had doughnuts and pizza and free-range unicorns. It still was unfair that they were all too busy to help me when I wanted to find Mr. Faboo, but were totally excited when Chip wanted to find him. My mind went back to watching Chip's fancy handshakes with the guys. There was no way around it—they just liked Chip better than they liked me.

"I don't have didgeridoo practice Saturday," Flea said. "Okay. I'll go."

Buckley whispered in Colton's ear. Colton listened, then said, "We'll do it."

"Splendid!" Chip said. "That's everyone! Let's meet at my house at precisely three thirty o'clock, Central Standard Time."

How many times had I told Chip that he didn't need to always say "o'clock," and that he didn't need to specify which time zone when we were all sitting in the same room?

"Wait a minute, wait a minute," Flea said. "It's not everyone."

They all slowly turned to look at me. My burger had formed a big lump in my throat. Even though Chip and I were friends again, all I could think about was how uncool and unfair it was that they were all so willing to follow Chip but wanted nothing to do with the idea when it was mine. I wanted to tell them it was fine by me if they all went together, but I was out, because they were traitors. I tried to chew and mind my own business, but I couldn't handle the stares. Plus, I didn't want them to find Mr. Faboo and be heroes without me. Not after everything I'd already been through. "Okay, fine," I said. "We're all in."

Mom was standing in Grandma Jo's room with her arms crossed, one hand holding a dusting rag, when I got home.

"Hey, I'm going for a bike ride with Chip and the guys on Saturday, okay?" I said, pausing in the doorway.

"Uh-huh," she said distractedly, without even looking my way.

"We'll probably be out until supper. It might get dark."

"Sure," she said in that same distracted voice.

"But it's a whole bunch of us, so you shouldn't worry."

"Yep."

I walked up next to her, crossed my arms exactly like hers, and stared into the same spot. After a minute, I said, "What are we looking at, exactly?"

She flapped the rag at me. "Oh, nothing, I suppose." She bent to dust the windowsill, but her head turned back to where she was staring before. She appeared to be looking at Grandma Jo's bookshelf.

"Nothing?" I asked.

"You see that trophy there?" she said, gesturing toward the shelf. I nodded. "Have you ever seen that trophy before?"

"I guess."

She finally turned to me. Her eyes were a little buggy and wild, like Mom was having a Close to Crazy Adventure. "No, not 'I guess.' Have you seen that trophy before or haven't you?"

To be honest, no, I hadn't seen it. But I also didn't really spend a lot of time in Grandma Jo's room. Mom was now tapping her foot at me and had her arms crossed again, and I was starting to notice a little bit of sweat on her temples. Mom was small and soft and sounded really pretty when she hummed, but make no mistake—she could be scary when she wanted to be. And, clearly, she wanted to be.

"No. I don't think I have."

"Aha!" she barked, making me jump back a step. She leaned forward and picked up the trophy. "Do you see what it's for? Do you see?"

I didn't want to, but I bent over and read aloud. "First place, Boone Raceway Street Stock."

"Do you know what that is, Thomas?"

"No."

She plopped the trophy back on the shelf. "Car racing, Thomas. Car racing. Someone took first place in a stock car race. Can you guess who that is?"

I didn't want to guess.

Fortunately, she didn't let me. "Your grandmother, that's who. But do you think she'll own up to it? No. She insists that she's had that trophy forever. Just like the tattoo. She's going out and racing at night, Thomas, I just know it. And I'll prove it."

I thought about the figure leaving my window the other night, leaving behind a racing bib. I'd had my suspicions then, but now I was sure. Mom was right. Grandma Jo was sneaking out.

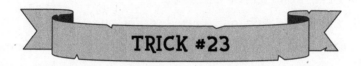

TRICK #23

THE SMELLY EARPLUG

The guys were waiting for me on Saturday when I rolled into Chip's driveway. The sun was out and it had warmed up a little, but it was still a chilly November afternoon. Owen had a GPS strapped to the handlebars of his bike; it was talking to him in a robotic voice, and he was tapping something into his watch.

"We should get moving if we want to be back before dark," he said.

"Everyone have their smithing socks on?" Chip asked, holding one foot out to the side so we could see the peach-colored socks he was wearing.

"Smithing?" Colton mocked.

"You are correct in your dubiousness. In the eighteen hundreds, a blacksmith would have worn a leather apron and trousers that would protect him from sparks and molten metal and flames and such. I'm sure we will see Mr. Faboo in such garb. It will be unlikely that he will be wearing smithing socks, although we can ask."

"Let's go," I said, and started rolling out.

Chip and I rode our bikes together pretty often. Sometimes we circled our block, racing each other. Sometimes we rode to Pettigrew Park to hang out on the monkey bars. Sometimes we went all the way into town to get ice cream. Those were my favorite times. We always played I Spy while we sat on the curb eating, and I always won, because Chip was awful at I Spy.

This was our first ride out to Old Midwest Town. As we got closer, the road became more gravelly, and fields of dry, dead grass opened up on either side of us.

It felt like we were the only people in the world.

"Hey, Thomas," Chip said, whizzing past me.

"What?"

He turned around and came back. "Why was the blacksmith mad at his boss?"

"I don't know, why?"

He circled back. "Because every time he made a horseshoe, he got fired." He laughed maniacally.

"I don't get it."

"You know, fired?" Wesley said, pulling up next to me. "A blacksmith had to heat up metal with fire in order to pound it into a shape. Good one, Chip!"

"I have one," Flea said. He had to pedal furiously to keep up with us. "Why was the blacksmith so cranky?"

"Why?" Owen said.

Flea grinned. "Because every time he went to work, he got a *pounding* headache." We all groaned.

"I've got one," Owen said. "What was the blacksmith's favorite kind of music?"

"Oh! I know!" Wesley cried. "Heavy metal!" He stuck his tongue out and pretended to be bouncing his head to loud music.

"Okay, okay," I said. "Why didn't the blacksmith's wife ever visit him at work?"

"Why?" Chip asked.

"Because every time she got near the fire, it would poke her." There was silence. "Get it? Poker? Like a fire poker?" Everyone groaned and laughed, and for a few minutes, it was pretty cool that Chip and I had the same friends, even if it did sometimes feel like they chose him over me.

"Dead frog!" Wesley shouted, pointing ahead. We all veered around a smashed blot on the road.

"Oh, hey, I have a song about that," Flea said. "I learned it at Scout camp." He started singing, and pretty soon we were all singing about smashed animals.

To be honest, it was awesome, and I almost didn't want to find Mr. Faboo if it meant we could keep riding our bikes together forever.

"Hey, Thomas," Chip said, just as we turned onto a dirt road that led to the Old Midwest Town gate.

"Yeah?"

"Do you think Mr. Faboo left because he was tired of teaching us?"

"Nah."

"I mean, we used his wig for spitwad target practice a lot," Wesley said.

"I don't think so."

"And there was that time we stole his Frida Kahlo unibrow and put it in Miss Pancake's hamster cage," Colton said.

"He wasn't mad about that."

"What about when we all made fart noises every time they said the word 'Texas' in that Alamo song he played for us?" Owen added.

I thought about it, coasting. "He was a little mad about that."

"See?" Chip said. "We've done a lot of things to Mr. Faboo. What if he's gone because he wants to be rid of us?"

True, we had done a lot of things to Mr. Faboo. But we did a lot of things to a lot of teachers. We wrote poems about stinky cheese for Mrs. Codex. We sculpted barf for Miss Pancake's realism unit. The only teacher we didn't mess with was Coach Abel, because he was the one teacher who could make us do stuff like run laps or drop for push-ups. But

everyone else was fair game. And Mr. Faboo seemed to have a good sense of humor about it. He never really got mad. He had never, ever yelled at any of us.

"No, Chip," I said, going back to peddling. "Mr. Faboo is a good sport. Who knows why he's gone? I just know we have to get him back."

2

The parking lot, which was just a field that had been mowed kind of short, had a few cars in it. We parked our bikes by a row of dead corn plants and headed to the front gate, excited about what we might see inside, because festivals were exciting, even when we were there on a totally non-festival mission.

"Hello, fellas," the man at the gate said. "Coming to enjoy the fair?"

Wesley stepped up. "Yes, sir. We'uns hopin' to get a look-see at yer blacksmith thar."

The man at the gate looked stunned. "I don't . . . I don't know what you just said. Brochure?" He held out a pamphlet. Wesley took it and tipped an imaginary hat.

"We were hoping to talk to your blacksmith," I said. "He's our teacher."

The man brightened. "Well, sure! You come right on in and have a gab at him." We started to walk, but stopped abruptly when the man's outstretched hand bumped Colton's chest. "That'll be three dollars each."

"We don't have any money," Buckley said.

"Oh; then I'm afraid I can't let you kids in."

"But we'll only be a minute," I said.

"Well, technically, that wouldn't be possible, as we wouldn't even be able to get to the blacksmith shop within one minute," Chip said.

"Five minutes, tops," I said, reminding myself to give Chip a death glare later.

The man shook his head mournfully. "Sorry. If it was up to me, I'd let everyone in for free, but it's not my rule."

"I promise we will just go straight there and straight back," I said. "Please?"

Owen was tapping the screen on his smartphone. "Oh. You guys. We missed it. It's right here on the website. Three dollars admission."

"You mean we're not even going in? I could have been home practicing my didgeridoo this whole time?" Flea asked.

I let out a sigh. "Okay. Everyone empty your pockets. We'll just send in however many of us we can afford."

Everyone reached into their pockets and produced a variety of treasures—Colton a slingshot; Buckley a handful of rocks; Flea a leftover cookie and an anonymous love note from Samara Lee that he was supposed to give to Dawson

Ethan in band and forgot. Owen's pockets were filled with flash drives—nine of them, to be exact. Wesley was carrying a Gatorade cap, two seashells, a folded piece of paper that had been through the wash and was now blank, a cell phone, a pencil stub, and his spitwad straw. My pockets were completely empty.

Not one of us had even a nickel, much less three dollars.

"Seriously, you guys?" I asked. "Nothing at all?"

"I had an overdue book fine," Flea said sadly.

I turned back to the man at the gate. "Are you sure you can't just let one of us in for five minutes?"

"Sorry, son."

I sighed. "Can you at least send a message to the blacksmith? Can you tell him his students want him to come back?"

"Tell him that his substitute doesn't even like history," Colton suggested.

"And that he's making us write papers," Buckley added.

"And we don't dress up at all anymore," Wesley said sadly.

"Actually, that part I'm okay with," I said. "Especially the pantyhose."

"They're leggings," all of them said at the same time.

"Whatever. Tell him that we got detention for no good reason," I said.

"Well, technically, we did damage school property. Very important school property, at that," Chip said.

Correction: I owed Chip two death glares.

"Just tell him, okay?" I said.

The man at the gate nodded, looking like he wouldn't remember a single word of what he was supposed to tell Mr. Faboo. "Okay, sure. I'll see if I can catch him on his break," he said.

We thanked him and headed back toward our bikes, Colton and Buckley punching each other in the arm and laughing, Owen showing Flea a music app that actually included a didgeridoo sound, and Wesley practicing his western walk, which looked a little bit like the way Grandma Jo walked that time she accidentally sat in Erma's Jell-O.

"Well, we tried," Chip said. We cut between two cars and skirted the log fence that separated the parking lot from the pasture. "We can probably think of another way to get to him. Perhaps we can find out where he grocery shops . . ." He shaded his eyes with one hand and gazed across the pasture toward the church at the other side. There were two kids playing in the churchyard, and another sitting on top of the fence and staring across at us. "I could probably find out where he takes his dry cleaning."

Wait a minute. Fence. Pasture. Kids. Church. The only thing separating us from Mr. Faboo was a field.

"No," I said. Chip walked on a few steps before realizing I'd stopped. I pointed across the pasture. "We can still get to him."

Chip gazed across the pasture with me. "Send carrier pigeons?"

"What? No. Who would do that?"

"Seemed more practical than smoke signals. Although I suppose we could investigate the telegraph if we want to remain historically accurate."

I put my arm around his shoulder, mostly to shut him up, and turned him so we were both looking over the pasture. "I was thinking of something a little more . . . sneaky."

He thought it over. "Invisible ink?"

"No, Chip, jeez. Sneaking over. Sneaking." I tiptoed in place to show him what I meant.

It seemed to take a moment for it to sink in, and then he took a deep breath. "You don't mean breaking and entering?"

"Well, I mean, no, I don't think anyone really breaks and enters into a field. But, yes, I'm thinking of just . . . sneaking over."

"Bad idea, Thomas," Chip said. "Really bad idea. That's stealing."

"It isn't."

"It is."

"It isn't."

"It is."

"Well, if that guy at the gate had let us in, I wouldn't have to."

Chip gave me a look I'd seen on Mom's face before. "You still don't have to. We can pursue the dry cleaner option. Nobody will think this is a good idea. Hey, guys—"

I didn't wait for him to finish. I walked over to the fence, slung one leg over, and scrambled to the other side. It was a low fence, and I didn't have to drop far to be in the pasture. In fact, it was only about waist high, but it felt like I was miles away from the rest of them already, especially since all their mouths were open with shock at seeing what I'd done.

"You should come back," Flea said.

"I'll be five minutes," I said.

"Don't do it, Thomas!" Chip cried, but the words were to my back, because I was already loping across the field.

Funny thing about fields—they seem small until you're running across one. I was out of breath, and when I glanced back, the guys seemed really far away. But so did the church. The only thing that didn't seem far away was . . . that . . . bull . . . over there.

I froze, one foot up in the air in mid-run. I held my breath; the bull let out a snort. I remained motionless; the bull dipped his head low. I tried not to blink; the bull took two steps toward me.

I let out a throat-ripping scream and bolted. The bull let out a snort and followed.

I ran like I'd never run before in my life. Part of me was

wishing Coach Abel was there to see it—maybe he would be so impressed he would let me out of ballroom dancing. Maybe he would tell his college coach friends and I would get a track-and-field scholarship and—

My foot hit a rock. Of all things to be out in the middle of a field. A rock. Everything happened in slow motion. I made *yuh yuh yuh* sounds, my arms wheeling. The bull's hooves thundered behind me. The cow pie that was exactly face-length away got closer, and closer, and closer. I had just enough time to glance at the guys, whose faces were all big *O*'s of surprise.

I managed to turn my head at the last moment, so at least it was only my ear that got plugged with things I don't even want to think about, and not my mouth. *Splat.*

But at the moment, all I could think about was the bull. The bull that was still coming at me, or at least I thought that was what I was hearing out of my one good ear. I pushed myself up onto my hands and feet and scrambled to get away, my shoes sliding in the same mess that was covering the side of my head.

Just as I got my footing and started to run toward the fence again, I noticed the bull take a hard turn to the left. I didn't stop, but I looked over my shoulder.

Sure enough, there was Chip Mason, waving his arms and yelling, "Hah! Hah!" and then running like the dickens as the bull turned its attention from me to him. Chip sprinted,

knees high-kicking, all the way to the fence line and cata-
pulted over it like a track star. The bull stopped short of the
fence and huffed and snorted in frustration.

I slow-jogged to the fence where the rest of the guys were
waiting, then slowly climbed it. When I dropped to the other
side, they all took a step back, looks of revulsion on their
faces.

Owen pointed at the side of my face. "Dude, you fell
in a—"

"I know what I fell in," I snapped. I whipped off my shirt
and began scrubbing my cheek and ear, gagging every couple of seconds. The ride home was going to be freezing, but
I would rather go home with frostbite than with cow patty
on my face.

Chip joined us, breathing heavily, his cheeks pink and
exhilarated. "Wow, when that bull has to go, he has to go,"
he said.

And that was all it took for the guys to burst into raucous
laughter.

"Let's just leave," I said. I had already started shivering,
but still I sank my shirt deep into a trash bin when we walked
by. "By the way, thanks, Chip," I said.

He waved me off. "Oh, no problem. I learned a thing or
two from your grandma. It was nice to get a chance to try
out my skills. She'll be happy to hear they worked."

I should have known.

"And we didn't even get to see Mr. Faboo," I said.

"I know," Chip added mournfully. "I had a whole list of smithing questions to pose to him, too."

"That's not why . . . Never mind."

"We'll just come back another time," he said brightly. "I'm sure we can borrow the admission fee from my mom."

"I don't know," I said. "I'll think about it." Chip wasn't the kind of guy who would understand this, but it was hard to make yourself want to go back to a place when you were leaving with cow patty in your ear.

We saddled up on our bikes and waited for Chip to put on his elbow pads and kneepads. The ride home was mostly silent except for Colton and Buckley, who told every cow-poop joke they could think of. I just

tried to concentrate on not freezing to death while the cold air drove through me.

We got back to Chip's house, and he invited us all in for hot chocolate. "Except maybe you'd like to shower first?" he suggested to me. "My mom is surprisingly patient with a lot of messes, but perhaps not that particular kind of mess around the kitchen."

I shrugged and walked my bike back across the street. I wasn't in the mood to toast with anyone anyway.

Just as I opened my garage door, I heard a surprised yell. I turned back to see Buckley pull something out of his back pocket and hold it up in the air.

"Look at that! Twenty dollars!" he yelled. "We could have gone in after all."

I pursed my lips and pushed my bike inside, trying not to notice the slapping and snapping sounds of Chip and Wesley doing their secret handshake.

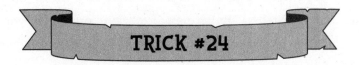

TRICK #24

AN EXPLOSIVE ILLUSION

The next day, I woke up to cold again. My window was open, and when I went to close it, my suspicions were finally confirmed. A butterscotch candy, the kind Grandma Jo kept in her pockets at all times, was lying on the windowsill, half in and half out of the window. I picked it up and rushed downstairs.

Grandma Jo was watching TV, her usual solitaire game laid out on the TV tray in front of her.

"Where's Mom?" I asked.

Grandma Jo motioned toward the kitchen. "Last I saw, she was making oatmeal for your sister," she said. "If you hurry, you can probably get some, too. If you like boring old oatmeal, that is."

I walked over and set the candy on the TV tray, right on top of the ace of spades. Grandma Jo gazed at it, then went back to her show without so much as batting an eye. I picked up the candy and dropped it on the two of hearts.

"You can eat that as far as I'm concerned," Grandma Jo said disinterestedly. "But if you spoil your breakfast, you'll have to answer to your mother." She pushed the butterscotch to the edge of the tray.

I slid it back over the two of hearts. "This was in my room this morning."

"Okay," she said. She gave me a light shove with her pointer finger so that I shuffled two steps to the right. "You make a better door than window," she said. Man, she was good.

"I know you've been sneaking in and out through my window," I said. She finally gave me a steely stare.

"Oh, do you, now? And how do you suppose you'll prove it?"

I picked up the butterscotch and waved it in her face. "You're pretty bad at concealing evidence."

"I put that there yesterday afternoon," she said. I raised my eyebrows at her. "In case . . . a bird . . . got hungry." She matched my raised eyebrows.

"I also found your racing bib."

She sat back and crossed her arms. "Prove that it's mine."

"There's a trophy in your room," I said.

"It's always been there," she countered.

"I saw you get into a car with a racing helmet on." I crossed my arms to match hers.

We stared each other down. Her eyes narrowed and her nose twitched. "Okay, kid. What do you want?"

"Nothing," I said. Again, she raised her eyebrows at me. "For now," I added.

"That's what I thought," she said. "So you want your owesies on retainer."

"I don't know what that means."

She scooped up her cards and sifted them into a tidy deck, then began casually shuffling them. "It means if I want you to keep my secret—and I do—then I owe you one."

"Oh. Yeah. That."

"Noted. Anything else?"

"Just . . . why are you sneaking around in the first place?"

She began laying out her cards again. "Because if your mother had her way, I would never leave the house except to drink tea and read books and make quilts. She'll never understand the exhilaration of feeling the wind in your hair as you fly down a stretch of drag track or the excitement of engines revving so hard and loud you can feel it in your teeth. To her, that stuff is dangerous. To me, it's what makes me want to get out of bed every morning."

"Why don't you just tell her that? Mom is understanding."

We both snickered. Okay, so Mom was understanding

about almost everything—but not about Grandma Jo's need for adventure. Or anything even slightly dangerous.

"Your Grandpa Rudy spent his whole life making things disappear and tying himself in knots and doing water escapes. How could I go from that life to the one your mother would have me lead?"

I supposed she couldn't. That was one of the things I loved about magic—there was a certain level of daring to most of it. Maybe, in a way, I was just like Grandma Jo. Even if on the outside I was kind of a chicken, on the inside I liked adventures.

"So I will owe you one, young man," Grandma Jo said. "But I will also continue to use your window. Barf and the others will be here tonight. There's a demolition derby going on over in Winville." She stretched out her arms like she was holding onto a steering wheel, then made car noises with her mouth, acting like she was crashing into things. "I'm the reigning champ," she whispered. "I have to go defend my title. But if you don't keep my secret, I'll be stuck listening to golden oldies radio in my room tonight instead."

I tried to imagine Grandma Jo being happy doing something like that, and I just couldn't. Grandma Jo would never be a golden-oldies type of grandma.

"Your secret's safe with me," I said. I popped the butter-scotch into my mouth and headed off to find breakfast. "I'll let you know when I need payback."

I was halfway through a homemade blueberry muffin when the doorbell rang. I heard Erma's bare feet slap on the entryway floor and the door open.

"Thomas! It's for you," she yelled, and I was surprised that she didn't add any sort of insult to it. Erma liked Chip—or, as she was known to call him once or twice, Chippy Wippy—but she wasn't afraid to call me a name when Mom and Dad weren't around. Maybe Erma was growing up a little.

I shoved the rest of the muffin into my mouth and headed toward the front door.

"It's about time," Erma said. She grinned and added, "Cow-pie face."

Nope, not growing up at all.

I wiped the side of my face and stuck my hand in her hair. She squealed and ran away. Of course, my face had been completely cleaned of cow pie for a whole day, but even just the thought of cow pies was enough to make fifth-grade girls scream. To Erma, my head was probably forever cow pied.

Chip wasn't alone. All the guys were standing behind him. Colton and Buckley were giggling. I scowled.

"Hey, Thomas," Chip said. "You want to come over?"

"No," I said, and started to close the door. Chip reached out and held the door open.

"But I have another lead."

"No offense, Chip, but your leads stink." At the word

"stink," Buckley and Colton howled, and even Wesley, Flea, and Owen cracked smiles. "Ha ha, yes, I said 'stink.' Your leads stink like cow poo, okay?" I started to close the door again, but Chip continued to hold it open.

"It's a very good lead," he said.

"No thanks. I think I'm done searching for Mr. Faboo." This was news to me, and I hadn't really thought it through yet, but maybe just accepting Mr. Smith would be less bad than what I'd have to go through to get rid of him.

Wesley gasped. "You mean you've given up?" He pantomimed fainting, dropping all the way to the ground with the back of his hand held across his forehead. He lay on the porch with his tongue hanging out.

"Mr. Smith is probably really nice once you get to know him," I said. They gaped at me. "And I like brown. And vests. Pantyhose itch and are always falling down." That last part was true. "And research papers can be really exciting to write."

Even I didn't believe that one.

"Come on, man," Flea said. "Mr. Smith won't even let me bring my didgeridoo into the classroom."

"Yeah," Owen agreed. "And he told me I could have only one computer at my desk. And he made me take off my satellite hat." He pointed to his head, which was covered with a spaghetti strainer.

"And he won't recite Shakespeare with me," Wesley said

from the ground, although he didn't open his eyes, and when he was done speaking, he let his tongue loll out again.

"We need to find Mr. Faboo," Flea said.

"And we need your help to find him," Owen agreed.

"Sorry, guys; not today." I wrestled the door away from Chip and began closing it. "You'll have to continue the revolution without me. I'm out."

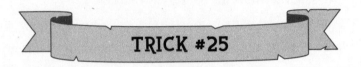

TRICK #25

THE STINK BOMB

On Monday morning, things were back to normal.

Chip and Erma were leading a small group in a ballroom dance on the lawn. They were all wearing matching socks—ballroom dancing socks, no doubt.

Patrice Pillow sat in her usual morning spot under the weeping willow, peering through the bare branches with a pencil and a pad of paper. Every so often she would get a wicked look on her face and hurriedly write something down.

Dawson was handing out homemade doughnuts, while Cecily juggled three potted plants nearby. Hilly and Milly stood on the school steps and talked to each other in acrostic, which meant I had absolutely no idea what they were saying. Stephen had strung a high wire atop the greenhouse roof and was casually sauntering across it with his eyes closed while drinking a cup of tea.

Miss Munch was carrying the newly fixed and buffed Heirmauser head, and Principal Rooster appeared to be practicing miming. Either that, or he was actually trapped inside an invisible box.

Everyone seemed to be doing their own thing, and I probably should have used that time to work on some magic.

Instead, I decided to slip behind the bushes to see if Reap was around.

"Hey, Reap?" No answer. "You there?" Nothing.

I crouch-walked to the spot where he was always sitting. There were a couple of hunks of bread, which told me he'd been there recently, but now he was gone. I pawed at the bush a little until I saw movement inside. Two beady little eyes peered out at me.

I picked up a piece of bread and waved it at the bush.

"Here, buddy. Come and get it."

The eyes didn't move, so I waved the bread again.

"Come on, now. You know you want it. No?"

There was a slight shifting forward in the bush, and my heart leapt into my throat. Wouldn't Reap be so surprised to find out that his mystery animal came out for little old non-animal-language-gifted me?

"That's right," I said excitedly. "It's nice, yummy bread. Come out, come out. Have a snack."

There was another slight shift, only this time in the wrong

direction, and the animal's eyes got dimmer as it pulled farther back into the bush.

"No!" I said. "Don't go! It's just a little bread. You can trust me." I shoved my hand farther under the bush, hoping to entice it out with the sweet, bready scent. "Okay, if you won't come out, maybe I'll go in." I parted the bushes a little wider, and to my surprise, a second animal—a much bigger animal—came toward me. "Hey, look, it's a cat! Here, kitty, kitty . . ." But then the kitty came at me even faster, lunging at me with the strangest meow I'd ever heard. It was more of a chirp than a meow. The kind of chirp you would hear out of a . . ."Skunk!" I yelled, scooting back on my behind until I slammed against the school wall. "Not a kitty! Not a kitty!"

I shifted to the side and dug my heels into the dirt to try to scramble away. But the skunk was faster than I thought it would be. And madder than I thought it would be. And more determined than I thought it would be. Every inch I moved, it hopped toward me another two inches, mouth open and chirping.

And when I flopped over onto my belly to try to army-crawl out of there, the skunk saw its opportunity. It climbed over my back, leapt off my head, regarded me with its beady little eyes, and then promptly turned around, lifted its tail, and . . .

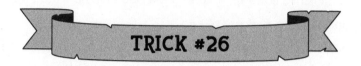

TA-DA! A TEACHER APPEARS!

Miss Munch made me wait in the parking lot while she called Dad to come get me. It was cold, and I smelled so bad, I couldn't even stand to be around myself. Not to mention, I was pretty sure I'd been in mid-scream when it got me, and I needed some serious alone time with a bottle of mouthwash.

"How on earth?" Dad said when he pulled up. He'd rolled down the passenger window, but when I got into the car, he rolled down all the others, too. "Oh, wow, pal. You reek."

"I know."

"What happened?"

Where did I even begin? Did I tell Dad about Mr. Faboo going missing? Did I start with the detention or talk about the bull encounter or mention the failed cupie? Maybe I should start all the way back at the day I turned that penny silver and Mom made me come here in the first place. Maybe if I started talking about everything that had gone wrong with me since coming to Pennybaker School, he would understand and stop making me go.

Of course, then I wouldn't get to have lunch with Chip or talk about movies with Wesley or cheat off Owen's fancy watch. I wouldn't even know Mr. Faboo was missing, which would mean that I wouldn't even know Mr. Faboo at all, and that was a really sad thought.

"I was feeding it and it got mad," was all I said.

"Feeding a skunk? Why would you do that?"

"Its eyes were cute, and I didn't want to dance with Chip and Erma."

Dad gave me an exasperated look. "All this to get out of one silly dance?"

"It's not silly," I said.

"Just dance with the poor girl," Dad said. "It won't kill you."

"It might." I crossed my arms and pouted.

"You know what will kill me?" Dad said. "This smell, if we don't get moving. Do me a favor and kind of hang out the window a little bit. Take the smell with you."

Even my own father was turning on me.

We drove for a while, and then Dad steered the car toward town.

"Where are we going?" I asked.

"To the grocery store."

Panic welled up inside me. It was bad enough to smell like a skunk in front of the kids at Pennybaker, but they were used to odd things happening. It was quite another thing to stink in front of the whole world.

"I can't," I said. "What if I run into someone from Boone Public?"

"They're still in school," Dad answered.

"What if they're out sick?"

"Then they won't be at the store."

"What if they have to go to the store to get medicine?"

Dad turned the wheel. "Thomas, I can't take you home smelling like that. Your mother will have a fit. We need tomato juice to wash the skunk off you. You can stay in the car while I run inside, but we're going to the store, and that's that."

Dad was a pretty laid-back kind of guy. But when he said "and that's that," he really meant it.

Times Dad Said "and That's That" and Really Meant It

1. **To Mom: we are not taking a Christmas photo in matching Rudolph sweaters, and that's that!**

2. To Erma: yes, you are going to clean that chewed gum off the back of your headboard, and that's that!
3. To me: plastic cups do not flush, and that's that!
4. To Grandma Jo: I will not distract my wife so you can parasail on Lake Jacomo, and that's that! (Grandma Jo did not agree that that was that. And her parasail was awesome.)

Dad parked right in front of the store and went inside. But it wasn't long before I couldn't stand the smell of myself. I got out of the car and sat on the hood, watching people come and go and counting how many of them fanned the air in front of their noses, and how many pinched their noses shut when they walked by (fifteen and nine, to be exact).

Only one man seemed not to notice the smell at all. He was holding a grocery sack in each hand; had long, kind of poofy white hair; and was wearing pants that ended at his knees, a long coat, and pantyhose.

Leggings. Whatever.

I froze. White, poofy hair, a long coat, and leggings? I looked again.

"Mr. Faboo?"

The man turned, smiled, and held out the bags he was holding. "Thomas Fallgrout!"

Before my brain could wrap itself around the severe uncoolness of what I was about to do, I slid off the car, lunged across the asphalt, and wrapped myself around his waist.

I hugged a teacher.

In public.

As soon as my brain caught up, I let go. Mr. Faboo was standing there, still holding the bags, looking surprised. And kind of nauseated. His nose wrinkled.

"Everything all right?" he asked. "You smell a little, um . . ."

"No," I said. "Mr. Smith wears brown all the time and makes us be quiet and read from the textbook, and he wants us to write a research paper and he doesn't even let us dress up ever and he gave me and Chip detention for no reason."

Okay, so maybe that last part was stretching the truth the teeniest bit. And maybe I couldn't believe I was saying that not wearing pantyhose was "wrong." But the rest of it was all true, and I meant every word of it. I was probably just excited that I had finally found Mr. Faboo.

I finally found him! All by myself! Sure, it was by total accident, and, sure, I was a little bit sad Chip wasn't there to celebrate the moment with me, but still.

For a few seconds, Mr. Faboo just stood there, the bags swaying slightly, his mouth hanging open while he tried to make sense of everything I'd just blurted out.

"I see," he finally said.

"You see?"

There was an awkward pause, and then he bumped my shoulder with one bag. "Well, buck up, little fella. I'm sure it will all get better with time. It was good to see you. Tell the guys I said hi. See you later."

He turned to leave, and now I was the one standing there with my mouth hanging open. He got at least ten steps away before I finally found words.

"That's it?" I asked. He stopped. "That's it?" I repeated louder. "I have been shot at, bruised my tailbone, been humiliated in front of an entire crowd of high schoolers, and I'm still cleaning manure out of my ear, all to find you and get you back, and all you can say is 'buck up, it will get better'?"

"You have what in your ear?"

"You have to come back," I said, ignoring his question. "Like, tomorrow. We all miss you. We can't take it anymore. We'll . . . we'll wear pantyhose every day." I wasn't sure if it was okay for me to speak for everyone like that, but I was desperate and saying anything that came to mind.

"Pantyhose?" Mr. Faboo repeated, looking more confused than ever.

"We'll all dress up as Napoleon on December second."

"You remember the day he was crowned emperor?"

I nodded. "Trust me, it's as much of a surprise to me as it is to you, but yeah, I do. And we'll be good. We won't ever complain again about anything. Ever."

Mr. Faboo started to look really pained. He came back to me, set the bags on the hood of Dad's car, and squatted down, his knickers rising to show his hairy knees under his tights. He rubbed his face. "I can't come back, Thomas," he said.

"What? Why not? Of course you can. You can just tell Mr. Smith that he has to—"

"No, no, I can't. It's not up to me."

"Sure it is." My voice was getting small, though.

He shook his head, and his eyes were all watery, like maybe he was going to cry. "I'm not allowed." He sank onto his bottom so he was sitting in the middle of the sidewalk in front of the car.

"What do you mean?" I asked. I was starting to have a squicky feeling. Something really weird was going on. Mr. Faboo wasn't the kind of guy who just cried for no reason.

He gave me a look, like maybe he felt a little sorry for me. Or maybe he was feeling a little sorry for himself and it came out wrong. "Oh, Thomas, you wouldn't understand."

"Wouldn't understand what?"

His head hung a little lower—any farther and his wig would topple into his lap. "I have to take a test."

"What?"

He leveled his gaze at me. "I have to take a test," he said, louder.

"Okay . . . ?"

"I can't do it," he said.

"What do you mean you can't do it?"

He gripped the front of his shirt, his eyes wide. "I'm not good at tests, Thomas. I've never been good at them. I get all . . ." He waved his hands around. "Panicky."

"But you graduated college, right?"

"Well . . ." He raised one shoulder and winced.

"You didn't graduate college? But you're a teacher."

"Pennybaker School is a unique school. It always has been. When I was a student there—"

"You were a student at Pennybaker?"

He gave me a surprised look. "Of course."

"What was your gift?"

"Well, naturally, it was history." To be fair, nothing at Pennybaker was naturally anything. For all I knew, Mr. Faboo's unique gift was dentistry. "Anyway, when I was a student there, we had a principal named Mr. Flockerbit. He was a wonderful principal, and he took me under his wing. So when I graduated, he sort of . . . bent the rules. He let me teach because he knew I already knew everything there was to know about history. American, world, modern, ancient, you name it."

"So he gave you a job."

Mr. Faboo nodded, his eyes getting watery again. "He did. And when he left, and Principal Rooster came along . . . Well, he never questioned it. I started wearing a lot of costumes so I would look older. Well, and also because I really like costumes. Anyway, it went on for so long, I almost forgot I wasn't a real teacher myself."

"So what happened?"

"Someone in the superintendent's office decided to organize our files, and they realized my file was missing some things."

"So they fired you? That's not fair."

"No, they talked to the state and worked out a deal. If I pass this teaching test, they'll let me get a certificate."

"Well, that's easy," I said. "Take the test so you can come back."

He stood and brushed off the back of his pants. "It's not that easy, Thomas," he said. "Like I said, I'm no good at tests. Why do you think I don't give them to you guys? I haven't taken one since I graduated from Pennybaker School myself. That's a long, long time, Thomas. I know I'll fail. So I'll just find another job instead. I hear they're looking for someone to run the gift shop at the museum."

I tried to imagine Mr. Faboo standing behind a cash

register in regular clothes, punching buttons and dropping pencils and plastic statues into bags. I couldn't do it. Mr. Faboo belonged in front of a classroom. Until now, this had been about me, about how Mr. Smith was boring and mean and driving me crazy with textbooks and research papers and detentions. But now it was about more than that. It was about getting Mr. Faboo back into the job that made him who he was.

I stood up, too. "We'll help you," I said.

"Oh, no, no," he said, dejectedly turning away.

I grabbed his wrist. "Yes. We'll help you. All of us. We'll figure out a way."

He patted my hand, then pulled it off his wrist and dropped it. "That's very nice of you, Thomas, but I'm afraid it just won't work. It was good seeing you." He picked up his bags and started to plod away.

I scurried around him to block his path. "It will work. I promise," I said. "It will work, and you will pass the test with flying colors, and the superintendent will have to let you come back."

He squinched up his nose. "Don't take this the wrong way, but you sort of smell a little skunky."

"Never mind that," I said. "We can do this, Mr. Faboo. You belong in the classroom. Who else could just walk into a classroom and start teaching history? You aren't just gifted at history. You're gifted at teaching, too."

He raised his eyebrows as if startled to hear such a thing, and then a slow smile spread across his face. "Huh. I never thought about it that way, but maybe I am. Maybe I have two unique gifts." He rubbed his chin. "I suppose it's possible."

"It's definite," I said. "Chip and I will help you. We'll get all the gang. Meet us at the picnic table right outside Pennybaker tomorrow after school, okay?"

"I don't know . . ." he started, but then he gave a weak shrug. "What other choice do I have? I don't even like museums. They're creepy."

"Great!" I said, launching toward him and giving him another hug. His arms stiffened at his sides.

"Oof. Yes. Definitely skunk," he said.

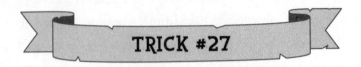

TRICK #27

THE PLAN PATTER

The tomato juice only helped a little. Grandma Jo wore nose plugs at breakfast, and Erma kept making gagging noises in the car.

"Bet you won't be tangling with any more skunks, huh, pal?" Dad said into the rearview mirror.

"Definitely not," I said, but I was too excited about the possibility of getting Mr. Faboo back to be sulky about a little body odor.

"That's what he gets for avoiding certain things," Erma said. We turned onto the long driveway that led up to the slightly leaning school building. We all tilted our heads without even realizing it, just like always.

"Avoiding what things? Is there a problem, pal?" Dad was glancing at me in the rearview mirror again, but this time I could see worry in his eyes.

"He's avoideeg ballroob danceeg," Erma said before I could respond. She was pinching her nose shut. "He's afraid of Sissy Cork."

"I am not," I said. I kicked the back of Erma's seat. She squeaked dramatically, because everything Erma did was dramatic. "I was trying to find my friend Reap."

"Who is also avoiding ballroom dancing," Erma said, then realized she wasn't plugging her nose and made a gagging noise before pinching it shut again.

"Surely it can't be that awful," Dad said. "Have you given it a try at all?"

Was it possible that he had forgotten the wedding incident? "A litt—" I started to say, but Erma shouted over me.

"No! And Sissy Cork is really mad about it, and he better hope she doesn't decide to arm wrestle him into a shoe box and ship him off to another country."

"If that country doesn't have ballroom dancing, I'd be okay with it," I said under my breath.

"What, pal?" Dad asked.

"I just haven't had time is all," I said. "What with all these chapters to read for History and the research paper to write and whatnot."

"'Whatnot' is code for detention," Erma said. "And he's probably going to get it again for stinking up the school. Smellyhead."

"Be quiet, Erma," I said, but part of me was worried that she was a little bit right.

"Whatever you say, Smellyhead. I wouldn't want you to put your smelly head on me. Smellyhead."

"Dad," I pleaded.

"That's enough, Erma."

We rolled up the driveway, and I had the door opened and one leg out of the car before we had even fully stopped.

"Whoa, pal," Dad said, reaching over the back seat like he was going to hold me inside. "What's the rush?"

"Dance lessons," I said as I scooted the rest of the way out of the car.

"That's the spirit," Dad said.

I glanced over my shoulder just in time to see Erma's skeptical, scowling face.

7

Everyone pretty much would have agreed with Erma's nickname for me, as they all stumbled backward when I walked through the hallways. They scrunched up their faces and waved their hands in front of their noses and made *whew* sounds. Even Mrs. Codex suggested I work on some independent study out in the hallway, which everyone knew was code for "Get that stench out of my classroom."

I caught Babette Prattle as she walked by, tossing a plastic hall pass into the air and catching it. From what I could tell, Babette's unique gift was gossip. She knew things about people before they even knew them about themselves. If you wanted news spread, you contacted the Babette Announcement System.

"Hey, Babs," I said.

She stutter-stepped, a look of revulsion crossing her face. She missed her catch, and the pass dropped to the floor. "What?" she asked warily.

I waved, smiled, and acted like nothing was wrong.

"Why are you out here?"

"Special assignment," I said. "On account of I'm so ahead of everyone else."

"Oh," she said, nodding. "Mrs. Codex made you leave because you reek like a wild animal." She thought about it, her head tipping to one side. "A dead one."

"Thanks," I said. "Nah, I'm just working on putting together this meeting."

She took a step toward me, narrowing her eyes. She looked intrigued. "What kind of meeting?"

"A meeting about Mr. Faboo," I said, then slapped my hand over my mouth like I hadn't meant to let it slip.

"What about Mr. Faboo?" she whispered.

I leaned forward over my desk. She leaned toward me, suddenly forgetting how foul I smelled. "Just between you and me."

231

She made a cross over her chest with her fingers. "You and me," she repeated.

"He can't come back to teach us until he passes a test."

She gasped, and I could just about see her brain trying to work out a way that she could make this between her and me and the rest of the entire free world. Just like I'd hoped.

"Is it bad?" she whispered.

I nodded. "He can't pass it by himself. He needs help."

"Help? What kind of help?"

"That's what the meeting is for," I said. "I have an idea. I want to meet on the roof at lunchtime. I just have to figure out who to invite."

"I'm on it," she said, not even bothering to let me finish. *Perfect.*

7

The roof of Pennybaker School was home to a greenhouse and to Herb Gardener, a twelfth-grader whose unique gift was horticulture. Nobody ever saw Herb outside the greenhouse, and since there was no planting club, pretty much nobody but Herb ever had a reason to go into the greenhouse.

It was the perfect place to hold a meeting out from under the watchful eye of Mr. Smith. Not to mention, we didn't want Principal Rooster to overhear our plan to help Mr. Faboo pass his test. Plus, secret meetings in the overflowing vines of the greenhouse were just kind of cool.

Which was the first thing Chip said when he walked in. "Secret meetings in all these vines are kind of cool. Oh, hey, Thomas. I didn't know you were going to be here."

"What do you mean you didn't know?"

"I knew Wesley and the howl pack would be here, but that was it."

"Howl pack? What in the world is a howl pack?"

In response, Chip tilted his face up to the sky—which was a lot closer in the greenhouse—and let out a long howl. A few seconds ticked by, and then three howls responded to his. And one buzz of a didgeridoo. The guys pushed through the door.

What the heck? My friends—*all* my friends—had formed a pack, and had left me out of it? I liked to howl, too, but how would they ever know? I was getting pretty sick of Chip taking my place in this school.

"You're letting out the humidity," Herb complained, rushing to shut the door behind them with a very worried look on his face.

They responded with more howls, which were deafeningly loud in the enclosed space.

"You guys are the howl pack?"

"Ow-ow," Wesley said.

"Ooowww," Flea responded.

"How come I'm not in the howl pack?" I asked.

"Oh. I didn't realize you would want to be. You usually

think things like this are dumb. You are certainly most welcome, sir." Chip bowed low. "Give it a try. Howling is fun."

"No," I said. "I don't want to be in any stupid howl pack, having to bark at the moon like a dog."

"We don't bark, good sir," Wesley said in his British accent. "We bay. There is a difference."

"And the moon doesn't really have anything to do with it," Owen confirmed. He looked up from his laptop screen. "Although tonight's supposed to be a full moon. Total coincidence."

I wanted to lay into Chip. Well, I wanted to lay into all of them, but especially Chip. *I can't believe you started a club without me,* I would say. *You don't even have club socks, and it's not okay that I know that about you and still don't get to be in your club.* I wanted to tell the rest of them that they wouldn't even have Chip for a friend if it hadn't been for me, so they'd better appreciate me. But when you started using phrases like "you'd better appreciate me," you started to sound like you were having a Mom on a Rant Adventure, and nobody wanted to let that guy into their club.

"It's technically not a club," Chip assured me, as if he could read my mind. Good. I hoped he could. My mind was making all kinds of ugly faces at him right now, and maybe even calling him a few names, too. "A club would imply a sponsor, membership dues, and regular meetings and bylaws, not to mention a quorum for voting. We prefer the Not It method, which works great for informal friend groups, but when it comes to official clubs—"

"Chip!" I clapped my hands in front of his face to make him stop. "It doesn't matter." (It did matter.) "It's totally fine for you to howl your heads off." (It wasn't fine.) "And you don't have to invite me to everything." (He didn't, but I wanted him to.) "Can we get on with our meeting, please?"

"Dude," Flea said, edging away from me. "The humidity is starting to bring out your skunkiness."

"Stolen skunkiness," I heard. I scanned the crowd until I saw Reap's familiar face, which was scowling. "That spray was supposed to be mine."

"Well, trust me, you can have it," I said. I got up and started toward him, lifting an arm—not because there was any smell in my armpit but because if you're going to wipe a smell on someone, an armpit is the best possible weapon I can think of. The crowd parted. Two girls squealed and jumped out of the way.

"Gentlemen, gentlemen," Colton said, stepping between us. I bumped into his chest. He looked repulsed and brushed off the front of his shirt. "Let's all remember why we're here." He turned to me. "Why exactly are we here, anyway?"

"Didn't you hear?" Patrice Pillow said. "Mr. Faboo is dying."

"What?" I barked.

"No, not dying," Samara Lee said. "Just moving to Antarctica to study penguins."

"I thought it was Africa, and he was studying lions," Flea said.

"I heard he's running away from a kidnapper," Colton said.

Suddenly everyone was talking over one another, all with different versions of what happened to Mr. Faboo. I turned a questioning eye to Babette. She shrugged. "You said not to tell them about the test."

"What test?" Wesley asked, and the whole crowd quieted.

I finally had everyone's attention, and not because of the way I smelled. "Mr. Faboo is in trouble, yes," I said. "But he's not dying or moving or running away from bad guys. He just can't teach again until he passes a test."

"So?" Owen said.

"So, he thinks he can't pass it. He needs help. And that's where we come in. We all have unique talents, right?" There was a murmur of agreement. "Well, I was thinking we could each use our gifts to coach Mr. Faboo so that he'll pass the test."

Now the murmur was much more doubtful.

"Horatio Oliver Williams?" Hilly asked. It took me a few minutes to work out the acrostic. H-O-W? Hilly wanted to know how she could help Mr. Faboo with the test.

"Well, you two"—I gestured to Hilly and Milly—"would be great with mnemonic devices." They looked confused. "Helping Mr. Faboo remember facts by using acronyms."

"Like, My Very Educated Mother Just Served Us Nine Pizzas," Buckley said. "Mercury, Venus, Earth, Mars, Jupiter, Saturn, Uranus, Neptune, Pluto. The planets."

"Pluto isn't a planet," Colton said.

"Yes, it is," Dawson interjected.

"No, it's not," Wesley said.

"Technically," Chip said, holding up one finger, "Pluto is a dwarf planet, which means it looks like a planet but really doesn't meet all of the criteria to be an actual planet. So you could change your acronym to My Very Educated Mother Just Served Us Nachos. Or, if you feel compelled to acknowledge the former planet Pluto, you could say My Very Educated Mother Just Served Us Nine Delicious Pizzas. The *D* standing for 'Dwarf,' of course. Although, now that I think about it, that might not really work, because every other letter of the acronym stands for a planet name, and 'Dwarf' isn't the name of an actual planet, nor is 'Dwarf Pluto.' So adding 'Delicious' to the acronym might be unnecessarily confusing."

Silence.

"You finished?" I asked.

He nodded. "Continue, Thomas."

"So you guys can help him memorize facts using your

acrostics. Owen can help him with computer questions. Flea, you can help with music history and facts about Australia. Patrice, you've got the creative-writing section. And so on."

"What are you going to help with?" Colton asked. "I doubt there's going to be magic on this test."

"Chemistry," I said. "That was what landed me here in the first place." For the first time since coming to Pennybaker School, I began to feel that maybe I *was* gifted in a unique way, even if it was with Grandpa Rudy's help. Lots of people can be given a magic kit. Not all of them can make water dance.

"You know, it's not a bad idea," Babette said.

Samara Lee nodded. "Mr. Smith isn't very nice. He made me put away my archery set. Nobody's ever made me put away my archery set. He said it was dangerous." She rolled her eyes like nobody had ever been hurt by a bow and arrow before.

"He gave me detention for dropping one of my bowling balls," Cecily said. "I was trying for five."

"And he threatened to call my parents if I didn't stop talking," Babette added. We all looked at her. "My unique gift is talking." Huh. So I wasn't so far off in my guess. "Auction-eering, actually," she added.

"He doesn't like musicals," Wesley added, sounding the most offended of all of us. "Not even *Newsies*. Who doesn't like *Newsies*?"

Colton stepped up onto an overturned bucket and pumped his fist in the air. "Thomas is right. We need to get Mr. Faboo back! Who's with me?"

Everyone shouted that they were with Colton and then began chattering about how each of them was going to help Mr. Faboo. Herb looked very nervous when we all began to file out of the greenhouse with our plan in place.

I noticed him spraying air freshener behind me.

But I didn't care. Finally, when it really mattered, I had everyone on board.

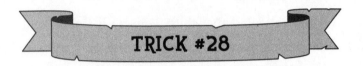

TRICK #28

A RIVETING QUICK CHANGE

Mr. Faboo came to the picnic table as planned, and we implemented our cram revolution, blitzing him one by one with facts and tricks and thermoses full of hot cocoa and fingerless gloves to help him grip his pencil. When it got so cold that Mr. Faboo's lips turned blue, Wesley figured out a way to sneak him into the theater through a backstage tunnel. We met in the empty auditorium, our voices echoing with algebra equations and facts about muscles and the names of different types of clouds.

Owen printed out practice tests, and Mr. Faboo got better and better, although his hands shook and a line of sweat appeared on his upper lip while he took them.

By the time he went home, it was dark outside and he looked exhausted, but somehow smarter.

"We're behind you, Mr. Faboo," I said, shaking his hand.

Chip leaned in to whisper, "Technically, you're facing him, so you're in front of him."

"I meant figuratively, Chip." Apparently some of our facts had leaked into my brain, too.

～

We moved on to the World War II unit in Facts After the Fact. Mr. Smith made us memorize European geography, giving us pop quizzes almost every other day to see how we were doing. We were all doing horribly. Except Chip, of course. He was really great at European geography. And any kind of geography. And any kind of anything, really.

Chip came to class in an interesting outfit. We all watched as he took his seat wearing a pair of wide-leg blue jeans, a denim shirt with the sleeves rolled up, and a bandana around his head.

"What is this about?" Mr. Smith asked as soon as Chip sat down.

We were all wondering the same thing.

"This?" Chip gestured to his shirt. "I was under the impression that this week we were studying the war effort on the home front. I'm Rosie the Riveter, the archetype of the strong working woman who flooded factories and other typically male-dominated career ventures because their male counterparts were 'over there.'"

241

"What does that mean?" Flea whispered to Colton. Colton shrugged.

"It means I'm dressing the part, just the way Mr. Faboo would want it," Chip said.

"Act After the Fact Month lives again!" Wesley crowed.

"I thought we weren't supposed to do that anymore," Buckley said.

"That is correct. You aren't. Mr. Mason, I would appreciate it if you'd change back into your proper school uniform, please," Mr. Smith said.

"I can't," Chip said.

"Pardon me?"

"This is what I wore to school today," Chip said. "My proper school uniform is at home."

Mr. Smith's cheeks got puffy. He let out a breath. "Fine," he said. "Tomorrow I expect you to be dressed appropriately, or you will have detention."

Chip's ears got red, and he looked a little like he was going to cry. Which was pretty unfair. A guy like Chip wasn't in it for the attention. He really did want to get into the spirit of the lesson by dressing the part. I didn't see why it was such a big deal for a guy to want to dress up.

I thought about it for a while, and realized that Chip was supporting Mr. Faboo in the best way he knew how. By refusing to let go of Act After the Fact, Chip was making a statement that he fully expected Mr. Faboo to come back. After all Mr. Faboo's hard work—and ours—we had every reason to feel optimistic about it. To expect it, even.

And just as Rosie the Riveter had supported the war on the home front, so had we supported Mr. Faboo on the classroom front. We'd banded together and shared our gifts. Now it was time for us to band together to share our belief in him.

I called Wesley that night, and told him to pass it on, starting with Babette.

The next day, I asked Mom if I could borrow some things.

"Sure," she said absentmindedly while she dusted around another new trophy. Grandma Jo must have been really good at car racing. "Do you see this? Do you see?" She pointed at the trophy.

"Nah, that's been there since Grandma Jo moved in, Mom." I had a promise to keep to Grandma Jo.

"It has not," she said, but her voice was soft and wondering, like maybe she thought it might have been there the whole time after all.

I caught a ride with Chip's mom that morning, and she said we were cute in our matching Rosie the Riveter outfits. She said she admired our gumption. She said we owed it to ourselves to get as much enjoyment out of our education as we could. She said we would probably get detention.

But when we walked into the school, we saw that Wesley had done what I asked. The hallways were flooded with Rosies. Even Clara the Poet was wearing an all-black version.

Principal Rooster and Miss Munch stood next to the Heirmauser head, smiling and clapping their hands and congratulating Mr. Smith on inspiring his students in such a creative way. Chip clapped his hands, too. He looked really proud.

Mr. Smith was super angry and told us to read silently for the whole class period. I guessed it was his way of giving us detention without giving us detention.

That afternoon, Mr. Faboo came back to the picnic table for a final brushup. We marched out to meet him, a Rosie the Riveter army.

"Rosalind Palmer Walter," he said, wiping the corners of his eyes. "The inspiration behind the Rosie the Riveter song."

"Just like you're our inspiration, Mr. Faboo," Clover Prentice said.

There was a chorus of "Yeah!" and "We believe in you!" and one "This bandanna's giving me a headache"—but we ignored that one.

"Thank you, students," he said. "You will never know how much I appreciate what you've done for me."

But he looked kind of sad when he said it.

Sad and nervous.

The next day was the test.

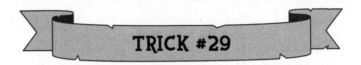

TRICK #29

THE FRIENDSHIP FLOURISH

I still hated pantyhose.

But a promise was a promise, and we had all made a pact to wear our Act After the Fact outfits to the testing site to support Mr. Faboo. I wrestled into mine, the whole time repeating to myself that they were leggings, not pantyhose. It didn't work.

"You're up early. Where are you off to?" Grandma Jo asked when I came into the kitchen. She was peeling an orange, dropping the peel on a paper towel spread out on the table in front of her. She had a black smudge across one cheek.

"My teacher has a test today, and we're all going to cheer him on."

"Today? But it's not even a school day." She was right. It was a Saturday morning. In my opinion, it was just mean to make a guy get up on a Saturday morning to take a test, but

Mr. Faboo didn't have a choice, so we didn't have a choice. She bit into an orange slice. "You must really like this teacher."

I grabbed a bag of miniature cinnamon rolls and sat across from her. "Yeah," I said. "I didn't realize it until he wasn't around anymore, but I really do."

"That's usually the way things happen," she said. "After Grandpa Rudy died, all I could think about was all the fights we had. Sometimes he was a real pain in my neck. Always off doing his magic at one end of the town or another. Leaving his socks on the living room floor. Snoring. Did you know that every now and then, when he was really tired, he liked to put his underwear in the freezer? Said it woke him right up when he put them on. Woke me up, too, to open the freezer for a bag of peas and instead find a crusty old pair of boxers resting on the ice cube trays."

I giggled. "I'm sure it did."

She popped another orange segment into her mouth and chewed. "The thing was, after he was gone, I missed that. I even kept his favorite pair of underwear and put them in the freezer. It was comforting having them there, in a weird way. It was sort of like that darn rabbit of his. The thing was always getting loose, and it aggravated your grandfather to no end. He talked and talked about taking it out to a field and setting it free. But then when it went missing, Grandpa Rudy grieved something awful. He looked for that rabbit forever. And kept his dish for a long time, too."

"I still have it," I said.

Her eyebrows shot up. "You do?"

"Yep. It says 'Bill' on it. It was in the trunk."

A small grin crept across Grandma Jo's face, like she was remembering something funny. "I guess I shouldn't be too surprised about that," she said. "The old softie. Anyway, what I'm saying to you is this." She took the bag from me, shook out the last cinnamon roll, and set it on the table in front of me. "Make this disappear." I tucked it into my palm using sleight of hand. "Now make it reappear." I did. She pointed to the roll. "As a magician, you're used to always being able to make things reappear. Now make it disappear again." I did. "And reappear." I did, but before it could even hit the table, she snatched it and stuffed it into her mouth. She chewed and swallowed. "But life just doesn't always work like that. Sometimes things are just gone forever, and you have to learn to accept it. So you have to eat the pastry while it's right there in front of you, because you never know if you'll get another cinnamon roll again."

At this point, I wasn't sure if we were talking about Mr. Faboo or frozen underwear or bunny rabbits or breakfast, but I had a feeling that Grandma Jo was trying to teach me a lesson about appreciating someone while they're around, because you won't know how much you'll miss them until they're gone and there's nothing you can do about it.

Which sounded exactly like what had happened with Mr. Faboo.

I wadded up the empty cinnamon roll bag and threw it in the trash. Grandma Jo kept working on her orange. "So you're off?" she asked.

"You want to come? You'd have to dress up like Betsy Ross or something."

She waved me away. "Nah. This day has nap written all over it. I didn't get much sleep last night."

2

The testing center was just a few blocks away from Pettigrew Park, so Chip and I biked there together. He kept losing his tricorn hat and doubling back to retrieve it, and my bike chain snagged my pantyhose and created a big hole right on the side of my leg, and it was so cold my nose was running, but we got there eventually. Owen, Colton, and Wesley were already there, dressed in their Act After the Fact costumes. They looked somber.

"Where is he?" Colton asked as soon as I hopped off my bike.

"Who?"

"Mr. Faboo."

"He's not here?"

All three of them shook their heads.

I went to the front door, cupped my hands, and peered inside. Sure enough, a dozen or so people waited expectantly with their pencils laid out on their desks. Mr. Faboo was not one of them. "Where is he?" I asked.

"How should we know?" Colton asked. "We were asking you the same thing."

More kids pulled up on their bikes. Patrice Pillow was dropped off by a car. Everyone was wearing their costumes. Unsung Revolutionary War heroes, sea captains, one James Armistead Lafayette—a slave turned double agent spy—and one writer named Judith Sargent Murray. Cars slowed as they passed us, their passengers peering at us curiously, as if this was the first time they'd seen a group of seventh graders standing around in fancy coats and bushy white wigs. Wait. I guess it probably was.

"Who was the last one to tutor him?" I asked.

"Not me," Owen said. "He got really good at Internet research, so he kind of didn't need me anymore."

"Wasn't me," Colton said.

"Nope," Patrice added.

One by one, everyone denied having been the last to see Mr. Faboo. Until I got to Chip. He was twisting his toe into the ground.

"What did you do?" I asked.

He shrugged. "Nothing."

"Chip. Were you the last one to tutor Mr. Faboo?"

"Yes."

"What did you do?" I repeated.

"I tutored him."

"On what?"

"On test taking."

"Oh no," said Wesley, who had just arrived. "That's not good."

"What did you teach him about test taking?"

"I simply told him that test anxiety is a very common occurrence, with twenty percent of students suffering severe test-taking anxiety, and sixteen to twenty percent more struggling with moderate test-taking anxiety. I reminded him that, on average, students who don't get a grip on their nerves score as many as twelve points lower than their confident counterparts. And, as we all know, twelve points could very well mark the difference between a passing grade and a failing one."

We all stared at him, our mouths hanging open.

"Don't worry," he said, his palms out to calm us. "I reassured him that he is in good company, as Abraham Lincoln and Vincent van Gogh both suffered from anxiety. I did muse, however, that perhaps it was Van Gogh's anxiety that compelled him to lop off an ear. Although the current theory is that he did it out of jealousy and fear at the news of his brother's betrothal."

We all continued staring. Chip started to look uncomfortable. He cleared his throat.

"Anyway, we discussed many anxiety-reducing techniques, such as getting a good night's sleep and being prepared. So he should be just fine. Ready to take on the challenge, in fact!"

I gestured toward the building. "Do you see him ready to take on the challenge?"

"Perhaps there was traffic."

"Or perhaps you scared him out of taking the test. He was already afraid, Chip. That was why we were helping in the first place."

"But I've always found knowledge to be calming. The more one knows, the more one is prepared to weather life's storms."

"This is not about the weather," I said. I heard Patrice Pillow snicker lightly. "It's about getting Mr. Faboo here to take the test so we can get him back in our classroom."

"Right," Chip said, looking thoughtful. "I suppose I should apologize, then."

"Well, I don't know how, given that he didn't show up."

Chip gave me a strange look. "We can just go to his house."

"Huh?"

He nodded. "We can just go over there and I can apologize, and we can all move on."

I leaned over Chip so far he kind of bent backward a little. If Chip was saying what I thought he was saying, we had a problem. A big, Civil War–reenacting, cow-pie-wearing, cupie problem. "You know where his house is?"

"Of course," he said. "It's the History House, right off the square."

"How do you know?"

"I learned it at the first Boone County History-Lovers Society meeting I attended." He pulled a scrap of paper out of his back pocket and unfolded it. An address was scribbled across it. "They gave me his address. I had my mom drive by, and, really, we all should have known that was his house by the way it's decorated."

"Are you kidding me?" I yelled. "You knew where he was all this time, and you didn't tell me? We could have gone right to him, and instead you had me cheerleading and chasing bulls and—"

Chip held up one finger. "Technically, the bull was chasing you."

I threw up my arms in exasperation. "Why, Chip? Why?"

His eyebrows came together in confusion. "Because we were having exciting adventures," he said, like it was the simplest answer he'd ever had to give. "Just like old times. I like our adventures. They're quite exhilarating." I didn't know what to say, but partly because I knew he was right. And that only made me angrier. "I should go apologize to him now," Chip said.

"No, you should make it right," I said. "Come on. We'll do it together."

The crowd parted as we saddled up on our bikes and strapped on our helmets. We took off, the air biting through my clothes and making me cold. Every now and then I heard Chip shout "Wait up!" or "Slow down!" or "My legs are getting tired." But I was pretty mad, so I kept going fast. It wasn't just about him scaring Mr. Faboo out of taking the test after we had worked so hard to get him ready for it. It was about the wolf pack and the secret handshakes and the dance lessons and the Heirmauser head. It was about Chip being more popular than me when I had been at Pennybaker longer. It was about everyone accepting New Kid Chip right away when they had treated New Kid Thomas like the enemy. And, yeah, it was a little bit about his "leads" always ending up being disastrous, but really disastrous only for me. He always came away exhilarated while I was hobbling and humiliated.

It was so many things, honestly, and I was really starting to think that maybe this was the end for Chip and me. We would fix the Faboo problem, and then we would stop being friends. He would go his way, and I would go mine.

I was officially done with Chip Mason.

Until I heard a crash behind me.

I skidded to a stop and turned around. Chip was crumpled in a heap next to his bike, which was lying on the ground, half on top of him, the front wheel spinning in the air. I let my own bike drop to the sidewalk and rushed toward him.

"You okay?" I asked. I crouched next to him, resting my hands on my knees. There were tears streaking down Chip's cheeks, and that scared me. I had seen Chip wipe out more times than I could count. Sometimes—such as when he was "conducting a crash-test study" on an old tractor tire that his grandpa Huck had left behind—he wiped out on purpose. I'd seen him take dodgeballs to the face and baseball bats to the back. I'd seen him fall off his bike at least a hundred times. And never—not once!—had I seen him cry about it.

He flailed a bit and then sat up and wiped his cheeks. "I'm not hurt in the physical sense," he answered. "But I can't help thinking you're angry with me, and I don't know why."

Oh. So that was what the tears were about. Ridiculous. I stood, placing my hands on my hips. "Why do you care?"

He turned his face up to me. He looked kind of pathetic, the way his helmet smushed his forehead into creases. "Huh?"

I let my hands fall to my sides. "I mean . . . you've got a lot of friends now, so why do you care what I think?" He looked at me the way I'd once seen him look at a wasp's nest— full of curious concentration mixed with a little bit of disgust and fear. I went on. "You're always dancing on the lawn or howling or making up a bunch of stupid handshake moves." I waved my arms around to mock his secret handshake. "The guys want to sit with you at lunch, and most of the time it's like I don't even exist. You took my head-polishing job, Chip."

His expression jumped into one of surprised confusion. "I took that job to help you out. You think the head is creepy, so I figured the least I owed you was to not make you have to look straight into its eyes every day."

"Sure, it wasn't about the glory of being the head polisher," I said doubtfully.

"No! Absolutely not! It was about helping you."

Well. That changed things a little. But only a little. There was still the matter of—

"And I dance to take the attention off you. You're the bravest person I know, so I figure if you're afraid of dancing, there must be a really good reason. Everyone is complaining about how you won't do it, so I thought if I held a few dance lessons, they would get so wrapped up in it they would forget about you not doing it."

That was actually kind of working, by the way. It had been days since anyone had bugged me about dancing. And I hadn't even realized Chip was behind it.

"And the real handshake was supposed to be with you, but you said it was babyish. I was just waiting for you to come around and choreograph one for us. And I was trying out moves on the other guys so I would be prepared for our own secret handshake. I even saved some of my better movements." He snapped his fingers three times, clapping his hands in between each snap, then tucked his hands into his armpits and flapped his arms like a chicken, chin jutting forward, then wheeled his arms three times, brought his palms together, and looked like he was praying. I had to admit, it was kind of cool to watch. "That's without the hips, of course," he said quietly.

"So you were doing all these things for me?" I asked, but it came out really skeptically. Maybe because I was really skeptical. Maybe being skeptical was my true unique gift. Maybe I could be a professional doubter. Actually, that didn't sound like very much fun.

Or maybe it was because sometimes it's hard to go from really, really mad to un-mad after just a couple of sentences.

"But . . . why? I thought you actually liked those guys."

A scraped patch on his elbow trickled blood down his forearm. "I do actually like those guys," he said. "I like them a lot. But they're not my best friend in the whole world, Thomas. You are. That's why I did those things. Because that's what a best friend does."

Correction: that was what a best friend like Chip Mason did. Best friends like me whined and got mad and stomped around and ignored and griped at their best friends. Which was not a friendly way to be a best friend at all. I was a rotten best friend.

But, man, I felt so much better knowing that Chip wasn't best friends with those guys. Which must have meant I thought he was my best friend, too. I probably should have seen that coming. What was it Grandma Jo had said? You have to eat your breakfast before it gets cold, because you'll miss it after Mom throws it away? Something like that, anyway. I had assumed she'd been talking about Mr. Faboo. But it turned out she was talking about Chip, too. Just like Grandpa Rudy didn't know how awesome Bill was until he hopped away, I guessed I just didn't realize how awesome Chip was until I thought he liked someone else more than he liked me.

"You're my best friend, too, Chip." I reached toward him. "And thanks for doing those things for me." At first he flinched, like maybe he thought I was going to haul off and smack him one, but then he took my hand and let me pull him up. "Come on," I said. "We've got to get Mr. Faboo to the testing center."

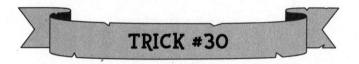

TRICK #30

THE ROOSEVELT RUN

Chip was right: it wasn't hard to tell which house was the History House. It was a big white house on the square, right beside the courthouse. One of the first buildings built in our town, it was at least one hundred fifty years old.

Chip explained that every month, the decoration of the History House took on a different theme. In the summer, it was the hippie movement, with lots of tie-dye and peace signs. In July, it was the American Revolution. This month, the theme was apparently the Renaissance, because there was a replica of the statue of David in the front yard, a Shakespearean hat on its head, complete with floppy feather. Telescopes adorned the front porch.

We marched up to the front door and stared at it.

"You should knock," Chip said.

"No, you," I said, suddenly nervous about being at a

teacher's house. This seemed like the kind of thing that just begged for a boring lecture or extra homework or something.

"It was your idea to come here," he countered.

"You were the one who scared him out of taking the test in the first place," I said.

"Technically, I just supplied him with some facts and basic information," he said, poking one finger up in the air. I grabbed his hand and slapped his palm three times against the door. "Hey!"

Fumbling and bumping sounds came from inside the house, and then the door slowly opened.

"It should be noted that my knock was performed under duress," Chip said before the door answerer could say anything. "I did not give knocking consent. Although, technically, I suppose it was more of a slap than an actual knock . . ."

I was too busy staring at the man standing in front of me to even pay attention to what Chip was saying. He looked like Mr. Faboo, only a lot more drab and tired. He had big, dark circles under his eyes, and his cheeks looked sunken.

But, most important, he wasn't wearing any kind of costume at all. Just a plain red bathrobe, with a pair of plaid pajama pants and a stained gray T-shirt underneath. He had a newspaper crossword puzzle folded and tucked under one arm.

"Thomas? Chip?" he mumbled, blinking in the sunlight.

He wrapped the robe tighter around himself and tied it to ward off a gust of chilly wind. "What are you doing here?"

"We came to ask you the same thing," I said. "You're supposed to be at the testing center right now. You don't even look ready at all."

He looked down at himself, as if to verify what he was wearing. "Oh. Yeah. I'm not going to that."

"Why not?" I asked. At the same time, Chip said sagely, "Your testing anxiety has gotten the better of you, hasn't it?"

"Chip. Shut up about the anxiety," I hissed.

"Not talking about it won't make it go away, Thomas," he said in the same sage voice.

"Stop it," I said through my teeth, "or I will make you go away."

"It's okay," Mr. Faboo said. He held up the paper. "I have this crossword to finish anyway."

I snatched the paper away. "No you don't. You have a test to pass so you can get back to your job at Pennybaker School."

He took the paper back. "You guys don't need me," he said sadly.

"Yes, Mr. Faboo, we do," I said. "You don't understand. History is boring; all those dates and facts and stuff. But you make it exciting. You bring it to life with your costumes and your stories about baboons. History just isn't the same without you."

"We need you," Chip added.

"That's really nice of you to say, fellas. But you'll move on just fine without me."

I opened my mouth to argue with him, but instead of words, a long beep came out. And then another. And two more. Followed by a lot of whooping and hollering on the street behind us.

Chip and I turned just in time to see Teddy Roosevelt rounding the corner on an ATV, complete with spectacles and a bushy mustache. He was pounding on the horn. On the back was Lewis Hallam, colonial actor, waving a white kerchief at us. Behind them was a long line of historical figures furiously pedaling their bikes or hitching rides on banana bike seats. Betsy Ross rode with Daniel Boone. Robert Smalls commandeered a Schwinn piloted by Thomas Jefferson. Unnamed colonists jogged behind the pack, carrying their hats in their hands.

I turned back around. "I don't think we will, Mr. Faboo," I said.

His cheeks were flushed, bringing some color into his sunken eye sockets, and for a minute I thought he might cry. The newspaper dropped out from under his arm and landed on his foot, but he made no move to pick it up. "What . . . What is this?" he asked, and he sounded the way I would imagine someone to sound if they found a softball-sized diamond on the sidewalk—like they had just won a huge prize and didn't quite understand why, but were pretty sure they were set for life.

"It's your class, Mr. Faboo," I said. "We all came out in costume to cheer you on when you pass your test."

"Just like we all came out to prepare you for said test," Chip added.

Mr. Faboo's eyes roved over the crowd and then settled on mine. "You believe in me that much?" he asked.

Chip and I nodded.

The ATV veered right, bumped over the sidewalk, and plowed across the lawn, going so fast, chunks of grass sprayed around us. It came to a screeching stop right at the bottom of the front porch. I blinked.

"Grandma Jo?"

Teddy Roosevelt winked at me and revved the ATV. "I hear someone might need a ride to a test? A very fast ride?" When Mr. Faboo didn't move, she got off the ATV and removed her helmet. Grandma Jo's white, curly hair looked funny with Teddy Roosevelt's brown mustache. "Listen, fella. As I said about a hundred years ago, it is hard to fail, but it is worse never to have tried to succeed." She looked proud of herself.

Mr. Faboo's eyebrows shot up. "Why, Theodore Roosevelt did say that," he said in wonder.

"He also said speak softly and carry a big stick. Now, I can go find a big stick if I need to, but I'd rather tell you softly to hop on and go take that test. You have a lot of kids counting on you." She gestured behind her. "The best thing you can do is the right thing, the next best thing is the wrong thing, and the worst thing you can do is nothing."

"How does she know all these Roosevelt quotes?" Mr. Faboo whispered.

"It doesn't matter," I said, pushing his back. "What matters is that you know them. You're going to ace this test." His feet started moving, slowly, slowly, but I kept pushing until we were off the porch and standing in front of Grandma Jo.

"Believe you can and you're halfway there," she said. She pushed a helmet onto Mr. Faboo's head and guided him onto the ATV. She hopped on, and the engine roared to life. She donned her own helmet, let out a whoop, and gunned the engine.

Paulina Rivers, wearing a tricorn hat and carrying a

lantern, climbed onto her unicycle and took off down the street, yelling, "Mr. Faboo is coming! Mr. Faboo is coming!"

"Technically," Chip shouted, holding up one finger, "Paul Revere didn't say—" His voice was drowned out when Grandma Jo throttled her engine again and spun out.

Grass and dirt sprayed Wesley, who had gotten off the ATV to make room for Mr. Faboo, but they were gone before he could protest, Mr. Faboo's red robe billowing in the breeze and Teddy Roosevelt's mustache fluttering to the ground behind them.

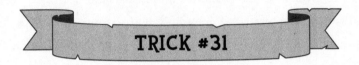

TRICK #31

THE BIG REVEAL

Chip and I perfected our secret handshake while we waited for Mr. Faboo to finish his test. It took a really long time. Way longer than we expected. After a couple of hours, kids started to get hungry, or tired, or cold, or bored, and trickled away. But we stayed. Because telling someone you believed in them was important, but sometimes you had to show them you believed in them, too.

"You boys need a ride home?" Grandma Jo asked. "I can swing you by on my way to the motocross circuit. Quad races tonight. I've got to pick up my partner."

"No, thanks," I said. "But don't worry. I'll keep your secret, just like I've been keeping the others. I sort of owe you."

Grandma grinned. "Nope; I told your mother."

"You did?"

"Yup. I figured it was unfair of me to make you lie for

266

me. Plus I was getting tired of sneaking out. Well, that, and she caught me coming in last night. Waited outside in the bushes for me. Like to scare the bejeebies out of me. I was impressed. She's getting good."

"And she's okay with you going racing?" I asked, even though I knew the answer. No way would Mom be okay with anything having to do with Grandma Jo and racing.

Grandma Jo grinned. "Who do you think my partner is?"

Whoa. Mom sure had a way of surprising me sometimes.

"If you can't beat 'em, join 'em," Grandma Jo said. She left, the buzz of her motor vibrating off the building for a long time. The only people left were Flea, Owen, Wesley, Chip, and me.

"Your grandma's pretty cool," Wesley said, watching her go. There were still bits of Mr. Faboo's front yard stuck in his hair.

"That was crazy, what she just did," Flea added.

"You should see what she does with a clown suit," Chip said.

"Huh?" Owen asked. They all seemed confused, but Chip and I just looked at each other and cracked up.

"Nothing," I said. "Inside joke."

The kind of inside joke only best friends share.

Not long after the guys left, Chip and I saw Mr. Faboo get up and feed his test into a machine. We waited while his silhouette paced nervously in front of the machine.

"What do you think will happen if he doesn't pass?" I asked.

"I suppose Mr. Smith will become our permanent teacher," Chip said. "Which means it will be likely that we will have more detentions. On the bright side, you'll be able to throw away your leggings." He pointed at my pantyhose, which now sported three giant holes.

I studied them. "Eh, I don't mind 'em so much anymore."

"I'm going to miss these shoes," Chip said. "They're making me look a lot taller. But it will be good to get back into regular socks again."

"Your vocabulary socks?"

"Yeah, those." I figured. Chip didn't have regular socks. Chip didn't have regular anything. "I did put them on this morning, just briefly, to learn the word of the day. Do you want to know what it is?"

"Actually, I kind of do."

"Stickybeak," he said proudly.

"Sticky what?"

"Stickybeak." He giggled. "It's used to refer to one who is nosy. Get it? Stickybeak? Nose-y?" He pointed to his nose.

"You made that up."

"No, I swear, I didn't. It has an Australian origin, and—"

The door opened and Mr. Faboo came out, causing Chip to stop mid-sentence. We both scrambled to our feet.

"Well?" I asked.

Mr. Faboo rubbed his even-more-tired-looking eyes and scratched his chin. He had left his house so quickly, he was only in slippers. The sun had gotten low in the sky, and it was going from chilly to cold. The wind kicked up his robe again, only this time he didn't move to fix it.

"Well?" I asked again. "Say something."

Slowly, a grin spread across Mr. Faboo's face, and then he raised his hands in the air, victory-style.

"I passed!"

THE FINALE TRICK

My throat was dry, probably because every ounce of liquid in my body had gone directly to my palms. My stomach gurgled, but I ignored it. Sissy Cork grimaced when I placed my hands on hers.

"No magic," she said, tensing her arms so I could feel how strong she was.

"No magic," I said.

"Okay, five-six-seven-eight!" Erma snapped her fingers in rhythm, and we started moving. I smacked my shin on the coffee table, causing Sissy to lurch backward and fall onto the couch. "Again!" Erma shouted. Sissy got up and grabbed my sticky, sweaty hands, and we tried again.

"You know, you're not really all that bad a dancer," Sissy said on our fourth or fifth try. "You spent way too much time being embarrassed about it."

"I'm better at magic," I said.

She shrugged. "I'm better at arm wrestling. That doesn't mean we have to be bad at everything else, you know."

"True." Still, I would have made myself disappear if I could have gotten away with it.

After we had successfully completed the dance three times, Erma pronounced us ready. Which was good, because in two hours we would be performing our dance for all the parents of Pennybaker School. Sissy went home, and I went upstairs to get changed. Grandma Jo was sitting in her bedroom, admiring her trophies.

I hadn't seen Grandma Jo too much since that day at the testing center. Since Mom had given her the okay to leave the house again, she had lots of making up to do with Barf and the others. With winter coming on, there was talk of snowmobiles and maybe even dogsled racing. Grandma Jo lived for the wind in her hair, and I was glad Mom finally saw that.

Except Mom did say Grandma Jo would freeze to death in a snowbank, and there would be no snowmobiling as long as she was around to stop it. Grandma Jo would never be done with her Fighting Mom Adventure. But she didn't seem to mind it so much. Sometimes I thought she kind of liked it. Maybe fighting Mom was an adventure all by itself.

Because I hadn't seen Grandma Jo a whole lot, I hadn't

really had a chance to thank her for what she did. Mr. Faboo was back in the classroom, and Mr. Smith was back to substitute teaching for Boone Public Middle School. We had a delayed Act After the Fact Month, and we were so happy about it, we went all out on our costumes. Instead of reading the research papers we had all written, Mr. Faboo had us turn them into screenplays. We acted them out with lots of drama. Mr. Faboo, in a new, super-fluffy white wig, sat on the edge of his desk and watched us with a big smile.

He also started doing relaxation exercises with us before each lesson, turning on soft music and telling us to close our eyes and breathe. Pretty soon all the teachers were stopping into Mr. Faboo's classroom to see what he was doing so they could do it, too.

We had our crazy strange teacher back, and it was awesome.

As soon as I got to my bedroom, I dropped to the floor and pulled out Grandpa Rudy's trunk. I opened it, lifted out the creation I'd finished the night before, and held it up to the light to study it. I smiled. It was good.

I took it across the hall and knocked on Grandma Jo's doorframe.

"Come on in, Thomas," she said. "I was just doing some sprucing up. I got a new one last night. See?" She held up a gleaming trophy that appeared to be of a woman swinging on a vine. I didn't even want to ask what that was about.

When Mom found it, she would flip, and it was just best if I didn't have any information to hide.

"I brought you something," I said.

"Oh?" She scooted over and patted the mattress next to her.

Hiding my creation behind my back, I sat down. "It's not as good as those, but . . ." I handed her the trophy I'd made out of Bill's bowl, Roosevelt's mustache, and a cinnamon roll. I had added a piece of masking tape and written across it: "1st Place Window Climbing." She gasped as she took it from me.

"Are you kidding? It's much, much better than any of those cheap trophies." She turned it in her hands to look at it from all angles.

"You'll probably have to eat the cinnamon roll. I'm sure it'll go bad."

"Well, we'll test that theory. This is a special cinnamon roll—the kind you don't eat right away because you're too busy appreciating it." She elbowed me.

"Thanks for getting my teacher back," I said.

Very gently, she set the bowl next to her swinging vine trophy. The doorbell rang, and I heard Erma's footsteps bound to open it. Grandma Jo grabbed each of my hands in hers. "I just provided the ride," she said. "You're the one who made him reappear. It was your magic."

"Thomas!" Erma yelled from the bottom of the stairs. "Chip is here for you!"

"Nah," I said to Grandma Jo. "It wasn't just mine." I stood and kissed Grandma Jo on the cheek, rushed to my room to grab something off my bed, and then jogged to the stairs. Chip met me at the top of them.

Before I could chicken out on being all squishy, I held out the socks I had gotten from my room. They were purple-and-yellow-striped, so bright I had to squint. Mom had chuckled when I asked her to buy them. But Mom knew Chip, so she wasn't really surprised. She even did that Mom thing where she put her fingertips up against her chest and said she was so proud of the man I was becoming.

"What are these?" Chip asked, reluctantly taking them from me.

"Best friend socks," I said. I pulled up one pant leg. "I have a matching pair. They double as vocabulary socks. Do you want to know what the friendship word of the day is?"

Chip looked from the socks to me. "Thomas, I . . ."

I continued before he could start crying on me or something, because that would be even more uncomfortable than what Mom had done. "Consonance. The word is 'consonance.'"

He beamed, squeezing the socks in his hands like he was afraid if he let up, they would disappear. "Thank you, Thomas."

"C-O-N-S-O-N-A-N-C-E," I continued. "You want me to use it in a sentence?"

He held up one finger. "Technically," he said, "the vocabulary word of the day is . . ." He trailed off, thinking it over. "You know what? Sure, consonance it is. Please continue."

We sat on the top step, and Chip put on his socks while I told him all about it.

ACKNOWLEDGMENTS

Writing a book takes a lot of help and support, and I'm so grateful to the people who help and support me. For that reason, Chip and I are pulling on our acknowledgment socks and going on a *Thank You Adventure*.

For Cori Deyoe, agent and friend, Chip has brought you a shiny pair of encouragement socks, because your encouragement is one of the best things about my writing day.

For Brett Wright, Mary Kate Castellani, Allison Moore, Ben Holmes, Sandy Smith, Oona Patrick, and Melissa Kavonic, Chip has brought you matching polishing socks for helping chart Thomas and Chip's adventure course and making sure they always stayed on it. In fact, Chip brought an entire package of hard work socks—a pair for everyone at Bloomsbury who worked so hard to get Pennybaker's antics onto pretty pages and into readers' hands.

For Marta Kissi, Chip is giving you rainbow-striped, sparkly, fluffy illustration socks, double layered with amazing talent socks. Thomas, Chip, and friends really come to life thanks to you.

My husband, Scott, here are your story hero socks, because you are the reason I write stories in the first place.

And to my kids . . . pick up your dirty socks. They're revolting! (See what I did there?)

Love you all!